Lainey Reese

Embracing the Fall
New York: 4

EMBRACING THE FALL
Lainey Reese
Copyright © 2014 by Lainey Reese
All Rights Reserved. This book may not be reproduced, scanned, or distributed in any printed or electronic form without permission from the author. Please do not participate in or encourage piracy of copyrighted materials in violation of the author's rights. All characters and storylines are the property of the author and your support and respect is appreciated. The characters and events portrayed in this book are fictitious. Any similarity to real persons, living or dead, is coincidental and not intended by the author.

Note from the author:
The following story contains mature themes, strong language, and sexual situations including F/M/F, BDSM elements and explicit sex scenes. It is intended for adult readers.

Cover design by: Regina Wamba, Mae I Design
Editing by: Nichole Strauss, Perfectly Publishable
Interior design by: Christine Borgford, Perfectly Publishable

Dedication

For my sister.
Rachel, you know me better than any person on this planet. We fought like wet cats, we laughed like drunken fools and we cried together like ... well, like sisters. There will never be anyone who means to me what you do, who can fill that place in my heart; it's yours Rach and always will be. I love you.

Special thanks to the Dom who provided me with insight and the pleasure of your experience to enhance the detail and realism in my writing ... I am grateful, Sir.

Prologue

October, seven years ago, Washington State University

"Oh. My. God!" Ziporah squealed as only an eighteen-year-old college freshman on date night could squeal. "Cami, you look so freakin' hot! You are going to knock this guy's socks off."

Cami turned a lovely pink and smiled at her as she executed a quick turn. She was dressed in a white linen dress that sported a delicate floral pattern, fluttery cap sleeves and complimented the curvy blonde's figure beautifully. She was soft and round in all the right places, and Ziporah, who was normally perfectly happy with her own svelte figure, allowed herself a sigh of envy. "Honestly, Cami, what I wouldn't give for a rack like that."

The rack in question was partially on display and flushed a becoming pink at the comment. "Wow, Z," Cami stammered, covering her chest with hands that shook just a little. "Should I wear a sweater? Do you think it's too low?"

Z laughed. "No, you idiot. It's not too low, and if you try to hide under one of those god awful bulky sweaters, I swear I'm going to burn them all."

Ziporah walked up to Cami and turned her to face the mirror they had hung on the back of the bathroom door in their dorm room. She slid her fingers through the thick honey-hued curls before resting her chin on her roomie's shoulder. "You are stunning. You are Aphrodite and Venus and Marilyn Monroe and every other sex goddess there is.

And you don't have to hide. You're beautiful and smart and funny, and if this guy has half a red blood cell in his body, he's going to be on his knees and following you around like a puppy dog for the rest of his life." Her slender tan arms wrapped around Cami from behind and gave her a big squeeze.

"Not likely," Cami retorted. "You've seen him. He has a lot of girls that he dates. He's not the settle down type."

"Not yet he isn't." Z agreed. The guy was all rough and tumble sports hero, and Z knew his air of wild recklessness was part of the draw for her friend. She had quickly learned that Cami only had eyes for the boys that were a little rough around the edges. "But one date with you and he'll be a goner for sure."

The two had only been roommates since the end of August, right before registration. Even so, before the first box had been unpacked, they were friends. They had made an instant and deep connection that made them feel like they'd known each other their entire lives.

They were complete opposites. Ziporah was pre-law, while Cami was studying music. Cami was a soft, round, blonde from a small town and shy to the point of phobic.

Ziporah was a tall, slender, brunette raised in wealth and privilege. She had what her half Jewish grandmother had called *chutzpah*, and she had it in spades.

The differences in each other delighted and drew the other, and the two of them were inseparable from day one. They squabbled over little things like Z's messiness and Cami's need for a minimum of ten hours of sleep. They texted during their classes, took all of their meals together and never questioned the bond that they felt would last for the rest of their lives.

"I still can't believe I'm going on a date with him. I'm so nervous, I think I'm gonna boot." Cami's hand fluttered to her tummy and held there.

"Don't you dare", Z admonished with a scowl. She knew from firsthand experience that was no empty threat. Cami's shyness and nerves had shown themselves in just such a revolting way more than once in these last months. "You got nothing to worry about. This guy is H. O. T. and he looks at you like you were made of candy."

Z gave her a wicked smile. "Speaking of which ... are you gonna let him have a lick? Or a bite?"

Cami's blush got brighter and she shoved away from Z with a grunt and an exasperated smile.

"Hey, just because you're a ho-bag, don't try to make me one, too," she grumbled without bite.

"At least I'm not a dried-up old spinster at only eighteen." When Z, who had lost her virginity to the captain of the football team behind the bleachers at sixteen, the way all good cheerleaders should, found out that Cami had been so shy she'd barely let boys kiss her, she made it her mission in life to get her friend laid.

Just as Cami opened her mouth to retort, there was a knock at the door and her mouth closed with an audible pop.

Z gave Cami's hair a final fluff and a wink to bolster her, and then turned to open the door. Mark Wahlberg stood on the other side. Not as cute as the movie star he shared the name with, but definitely cute. Blond, wavy hair. Blue eyes. A perfect melt-your-heart smile with straight white teeth, and since he was here on a wrestling scholarship, covered in muscles that made both teenaged girls' hearts flutter.

Z cocked her hip and put a hand on it for show as she sighed, "Oh, the babies you two would make."

"Z!" Cami turned fire engine red and smacked her nearest and dearest in the arm so hard she almost toppled over. Z laughed and rubbed her arm. "Just sayin'. Sheesh."

Mark laughed quietly. "She doesn't bother me, Cami. You look great." He smiled slowly at her and sent her an equally slow wink. Z snickered as she watched the effect it had on her friend. She seemed to melt where she stood, then smoothed her skirt and headed toward the door. Z laughed like a loon when Cami whispered, "Maybe just one bite", as she passed her on the way.

Twelve-thirty in the morning and Ziporah had gone beyond worried to scared. Mark had picked Cami up at six o'clock sharp. They were only going to dinner; nothing else had been planned since they both had classes the next day. Maybe she was just being a mother hen, but the Cami she knew was no night owl and wilted after ten o'clock. She also would never, under any circumstances, go all the way on a first date, no matter how cute the boy was, so the late hour was really bugging her. Z picked up her cell and sent off the fifth text of the evening.

It's super late C. U gotta call or at least txt. Worried about you grl.

Two a.m. arrived and Ziporah was frantic. And pissed. She was going to kick the crap out of someone. Whether it was Mark or Cami had yet to be seen, but someone was getting an ass-whooping. She was just shrugging into her jacket, having no clue where she was going to go to look for them but needing to look anyway, when the door finally opened.

"It's about fu ..." Her words tailed off in shock at the sight in front of her. Z's mouth just hung open while her brain tried to make sense out of what she saw.

A mess of a girl stood silhouetted in the doorway. Z let out a cry when she turned on the light. Hair that had been shiny and full of bouncing curls, was muddy and hung in limp clumps. The bright and blushing face that had smiled as she walked out of this room was bloody, bruised and swollen. Her lovely dress was as muddy as her hair and looked as though it had been fed through a shredder. Even Cami's legs were destroyed, covered in bloody scratches, skinned knees and bare, filthy feet.

All this registered in seconds, but those seconds seemed to last a lifetime for them as Z brought her horrified eyes back to meet Cami's devastated stare.

"He hurt me, Z."

Chapter One

October, five years later, New York

"Are you masturbating, Cami?" Cami flinched as her eyes flew about the room, trying desperately not to look her therapist in the eye.

"Um. Well, umm."

"We talked about this last week. You were supposed to try. It will help you take back your sexuality. Help you claim it."

"I know," Cami hedged, "I tried. In the summer and spring I don't have any trouble doing it. It's just hard to do in the fall." She looked out the window at the view of Central Park, with the trees clothed in bronze, gold and yellow. And hated that she hated it. "Too many memories." Too many similarities.

Mark had been a perfect gentleman during dinner. He'd flirted just the right amount and had also spoken to her like she had a brain. He was interested in what she had to say, and that had made her love him just a little. Her looks and shyness had always made boys assume she was empty headed, so when Mark had acted as though he thought she was more than a pair of boobs and a piece of ass, she hadn't been able to resist.

When dinner was over and he suggested the ride into the country to visit a local pumpkin patch and corn maze, she hadn't even considered refusing. They'd driven along the winding road, leaving the city further and further behind.

EMBRACING THE FALL

Cami had been quietly thrilled when Mark had reached out and gently taken her hand. He'd held it lightly and drew lazy tickling circles on her wrist with his thumb almost the entire way, and she had marveled at the riotous fall colors flashing under the street lamps.

When they arrived at the farm, Cami hadn't noticed Mark wasn't surprised that it was closed. No, she didn't clue into that until later. "Where are you going?" she'd asked, "it's closed."

"C'mon. Let's go through the maze any way. It'll be fun." She hadn't thought twice about it when he grabbed a blanket and a flashlight from his trunk either, because he'd wrapped the blanket around her shoulders and told her, "Here, so you don't get cold." She'd thought he was sweet.

Then he'd led her into the corn that was two feet above her and she'd giggled as they'd zigzagged through the field, with the stars over head. The moon was so big and yellow; it seemed as though she could reach out and touch it.

She had been breathless when he stopped them. They had made it to the middle, and with the moon shining down like a magical spotlight, he'd slipped the blanket from her shoulders so it spread at their feet, and kissed her. Slow, soft and as romantic as the rest of the night had been. One kiss led to another and then another.

Then she felt him urging her down to the blanket.

Cami steeled herself and placed her hands on his shoulders. She would have preferred that he know when to stop, not push it so far that she had to put on the brakes. But, it didn't dim his light in her eyes. It was college, and after all, he didn't know she was a virgin. "Mark," she murmured as she pushed a little on his shoulders. "Mark. Stop. We should go now."

"C'mon baby," Mark wheedled as he placed his mouth on her neck and sucked. "C'mon. You've been driving me crazy tonight." His hands snaked around to her bottom and he squeezed her pelvis tight to his erection as he ground against her. "You know you want to."

"No." Cami pushed a little harder, her passion fading fast as he kept grinding and pumping against her. Kisses that she had found devastating in their passion just moments before, she now found revolting as she twisted her head back and forth trying to dodge his relentless tongue. "Stop it Mark!" She gave up all efforts to be nice about it and shoved at him when he started again to pull her down to the blanket. "I said no. Take me home. No."

"C'mon. Christ. I'll make it good. I'll even eat you first." This horrifying thing was said just as he stuck one hand under her skirt, past her panties and speared two blunt fingers into her untried and never before touched flesh. Cami went cold inside and wrenched out of his arms with a feral screech. She didn't yell or hit him, she just turned and ran.

She hadn't gotten far.

"Cami?" Dr. West said in her quiet way, "what are you thinking right now?"

"About that night. About how I wish I could go back and never go on that date."

"But you know that isn't possible. So, what is possible for you?"

Cami looked at the sweet and gentle doctor and wanted to kick her. Not that she ever would, it's just that the woman was so frustrating the way she made Cami think for herself. She didn't want to think for herself sometimes. Sometimes she wanted ... ah, hell ... she didn't know what she wanted sometimes.

"I can focus on today. I can take the life I have and be glad in it." Cami repeated the mantra with all the enthusiasm of a third grader reciting times tables.

Dr. West smiled and wasn't fooled for a second. "Cami, have you ever considered exploring your sexuality?"

"Exploring how?" Cami was perplexed. "What do you mean?"

"I mean that you tend to hide from your own sexuality. You've taken on guilt and blame for what happened, almost as though you are punishing yourself for it. You turn away from anything that excites you or gives you pleasure." Dr. West looked kind yet stern when she leaned forward and added, "You have got to stop beating yourself up for this."

"I don't beat myself up," Cami protested.

"That comment about wanting to go back and not go on the date. That was a kick against you. Not him."

Cami opened her mouth to insist it wasn't when the doctor rushed on. "By that statement you are saying if *you* had done differently this wouldn't have happened. You—not him."

Nothing she could say to that.

"You went on a date with a handsome and charming young man who was nice to you. You kissed him under the moon and stars, and it was lovely and romantic. The rest is on him. Not you. And during the spring and summer and winter, you know this and never question it." She stopped for a moment and let that sink in.

"It's because the fall is dark now. From September till December, it's always dark for me. I feel so helpless when I remember it. Weak and stupid and helpless," Cami confessed with a tiny sob.

"You were not weak; he was a wrestler. You were not stupid; you were trusting. You had no reason not to trust. And the sad truth is that there was no one there to help you." Dr. West held up her iPad and scrolled through what Cami assumed was her file. "Now, I have more on that thought, but first," she continued, "let's go over what you did after. After this pillar of society left you battered and bleeding in a cornfield." Cami remembered.

She'd been in shock, so nothing felt real. Not the pain, not the endless wandering in the maze, not any of it. She'd stumbled and fumbled for hours trying to find her way out of that corn. When she finally had enough and just pushed through the walls of it, forgoing the trails, she'd eventually stumbled out into the pumpkin patch. She must have tripped a dozen times over the fat orange fruits, with their prickly green vines that shredded like sandpaper through her bare feet and ankles as she made her way to the house that sat on the edge of the field.

The poor farmer and his wife ... The farmer had raced out with his shotgun, looking for Mark, while his tender-hearted wife had cried for her. She hadn't let them call the police. It made her panic when they reached for the phone. Panic or no, they were insistent, but she managed to get them to agree to take her home to pick up Ziporah so she wouldn't have to face this alone. Then they took both girls to the hospital from there.

"I still can't believe he got away with it," Cami said in a whisper.

"Again, look to yourself and what you have control over. You did everything right. You faced the police and the exams. You faced the scandal and the long drawn out court battle. You did everything you could."

"But it wasn't enough. He walked away."

"What did Ziporah teach you to say?"

"Justice would rather see guilty men go free than even one innocent man go to jail."

Cami's skin still crawled when she thought about it. All that humiliation of the doctor's exam and then the horror of the cross examination by the defense attorney, only to have Mark found not guilty because he claimed it was the steroids. That he had no idea that his 'vitamins' were actually steroids and that he'd been blindsided by *'roid rage* when she tried to run from him.

She had sat there with her stomach churning, while he'd sat on that witness stand and cried. Looking at her with his perfect hair and perfect blue eyes overflowing with tears, while he'd begged her to forgive him.

Well, she hadn't forgiven him, but the jury had. They'd seen it as a terrible and tragic mistake— an accident. No prior trouble of any kind for him and no other girls had come forth during the trial to show any pattern, so the jury had let him go.

"He didn't get off completely scott-free. He lost his scholarship and had to leave school."

"Yes but his parents were rich and just put him in another school."

"Was that something you could control?" the doctor asked in her calm voice.

"No." Knowing that she couldn't have changed anything didn't help her feel any better.

"Cami." She leaned forward and placed her elbows on her knees, giving her an earnest stare, as though compelling Cami to really listen to what she had to say next. "This creep took something from you that you are never getting back. He took it in a brutal and unforgivable way. He stole that from you." She paused for a moment that stretched until Cami could hear her own heart beat. "What I want you to ask yourself is: how much more are you going to let him steal from you?"

Chapter Two

"I'm sorry. What?" Cami was more than a little baffled.

"Think about that. You date, but it's never for very long. The men you've been brave enough to have sex with, you pushed away almost before the sheets cooled. You close yourself down sexually, especially in the fall and you can count on one hand the number of orgasms you've had.

"He did this to you five years ago, and I guarantee he walked away after that trial and went on with his life. You need to decide that you are going to go on with yours and not give him, or his actions, even one more second of it."

Cami fidgeted and dug deep inside herself. There were things she felt, things that scared her to even think about, but the doctor was right. She needed to stop living like this. Stop living in this darkness and come into the light of day. She needed to face those fears if she ever had a chance at overcoming them.

"It's just that—" She took a breath and mentally grabbed her courage with both hands. "It's just that I only date guys who don't scare me." She peeked up at the other woman through her lashes.

"Go on." There was knowledge and acceptance in her eyes that Cami took hope from.

"They don't scare me, but they don't excite me either. I try to find gentle men. Kind ones, you know? The *'hold the door for you'* and *'wait for you to make the first move'* kind. But, I just feel cold when they touch me. Empty, and honestly, bored."

"Ah, now we're getting somewhere. Is that why you break up with them so soon after you've had sex? Because they're boring in bed?"

"Well, yeah." Cami felt like her face was on fire and was sure she was red as a beet right now. But it felt good to be finally airing this. She felt like she'd just uncorked a bottle and all the fears were gushing out, freeing her. "Before Mark, before that night, I liked the guys who were kinda dangerous, you know? I know it's super cliché for the good girl to lust after the bad boys, but that's how it was for me. You know that movie Fatal Attraction, with Michael Douglas? I watched that one scene, when he and the psycho shrink go back to her place and tear into each other, over and over again when I was a teen."

Dr. West was getting animated; Cami thought she looked like she wanted to get up and pace the way she shifted in her seat. "Cami, I have been waiting for you to get here for years. Keep going. You've almost got it. Tell me, what did you like about that scene? Why that one and not one of the others?"

Cami swallowed, afraid to say it, but more afraid not to. "Because he shoved her around, and ripped off her clothes. Because he forced her." The last was a barely audible whisper and the root of her shame.

"No!" Cami startled at the sharp crack of Dr. West's voice. "No. Cami, listen to me very carefully. This is vital that you understand this point. That scene was about consent. Aggressive? Yes. Primal and a little mean? Yes. But rape, it was not. They both knew what they wanted. They both enjoyed what happened. And frankly, that scene was hot as hell." That surprised a laugh out of Cami, and Dr. West sat back to look at her with an indulgent smile.

"Cami, I think it's time you and I start discussing your true nature. I think you are finally ready to face the truth of who and what you are."

"What do you mean? What am I?"

"Cami, honey, you're a sexual submissive."

Cami felt like she should snort or shrug that off some way, but instead she felt herself nodding.

"Do you know what that means? To be a submissive?"

"Yeah." Cami shrugged and fidgeted in her seat as she felt the heat of a blush wash over her cheeks. "I mean, I think so. I've read about them a little, you know, in romance novels and stuff."

Dr. West leaned forward and braced her elbows on her knees. "What do you feel when you read about submissives, Cami?"

"What do you mean?" *Although she was afraid she knew the answer to that already.*

"Do you feel a connection with the women in the stories? A sense of belonging or rightness? Or, do you find yourself put off by their actions and what is being done to them?"

She had to take two deep breaths before she could summon the courage to face this question honestly. "I felt connected. Completely. I always wish it were me." Cami swallowed and felt a panic attack building that she valiantly tried to hold at bay. "But that's wrong, right? That's awful. Do I want those things because of the attack? Is that why you think I'm a submissive now? Did he make me one?" Tears filled her eyes as she voiced the fears she'd been running from for years.

Cami hadn't realized she'd closed her eyes until they flew open when her icy hands were engulfed in Dr. West's gentle clasp. "No, no I don't believe that. Lots of survivors of violence go on to have what is considered *vanilla* sex lives. The attacks don't change their internal makeup or desires in almost all cases. Just as I believe your attack didn't change yours. From our years together, and all that I've learned about who you are, I can say with full confidence that you are a submissive and you are one, not because of what happened to you, but regardless of it."

"If you hadn't been attacked, you would have discovered this about yourself naturally. You would have probably had a couple of normal relationships before you started exploring. It is too deeply ingrained in you for you to have ignored it for long. But, because of what happened, you've run from that nature. You've buried it. I'm just glad that you are now ready to explore it."

"But, how can I be like that?" Cami felt the confusion and shame whelming up as tears filled her eyes. "How can I want to be pushed around and beat on or whatever after what happened to me? And if I do like that stuff, why didn't I like when he did it to me? Was I asking for it really and then just didn't like what I got?" That last humiliating thought had been haunting her for years and to speak it out loud, for the first time, was like a knife in her heart. Cami covered her face with both hands and cried softly into them.

"Cami." The doctor's voice was soothing and full of compassion. "There is a huge difference between BDSM and what was done to you. You had no control in what happened to you, you were taken against your will and you were hurt out of cruelty. In the BDSM community, that would never happen. Every single person in that lifestyle is supposed to live by a code of honor. Safe. Sane. And consensual. There are safe words that a submissive has that are there for them to stop any activity, at any time, completely. The Dominant may be handling the whip or meting out some other pseudo-punishment, but the person who has the true power in any Dom/sub relationship is the submissive. They can halt everything by simply uttering a single word."

Cami dropped her hands and felt the cold and exposed wounds within her start to heal. Like the sun was shining on her dark places for the first time, and that warmth brought the promise of peace.

"Being a submissive is more than you think. It's more than just sex for people that have it as deeply ingrained as you do." Dr. West smiled kindly at her and Cami sat a little straighter, as there wasn't judgment in her expression or revulsion, only the same calm compassion that she'd always shown. "Hit the internet. Research. Not just fiction, but look for actual active groups and also read some articles and non-fiction books on this lifestyle. Explore this part of yourself and embrace it. Take back your life Cami. Take back the joy you would have had if this had never happened."

Chapter Three

October, today, New York

"Evan." Evan's assistant Tanner stuck his head in the door. "You got a visitor. You got time for a break, or should I have her come back later?"

Evan looked up from the spreadsheet he was studying. His mind was jumbled with percentages, costs and gross vs. net profits, so he almost told Tanner to send the visitor away out of hand.

"Who is it?" he asked instead, checking his watch. It was barely nine in the morning, so he was curious as to who would come calling so early in the work day.

"Zoe Hollister." A smile broke out on Evan's face and he was glad he'd asked first.

"Send her in, Tanner." As he was pushing up from his desk, Zoe came tumbling into his office as bubbly and happy as a puppy.

"Evan!" She was stunning in her beauty. Raven hair and impossibly large blue eyes. She had a figure he knew, in intimate detail, was worthy of a mythical goddess and a rich sensuality that could bring lesser men to their knees.

She was also filled with an exuberant and precocious personality that spread joy wherever she went. Zoe was on her way to becoming a veterinarian, and with her boundless energy and her love of all things furry, it was the perfect fit for her.

"What a nice surprise, pet." He caught her in a hug and held her close for a brief moment as pure affection filled his heart and brought warmth and contentment to his otherwise stressful morning.

"I am so sorry to interrupt you at work, but I just had to talk to you alone." As she stepped back and he guided her to one of the leather seats facing his desk, he saw her smile falter. Rather than sitting back at his desk, he took the remaining seat and held her hand.

"What is it, Zoe?" He braced himself against letting his mind jump to possibilities and waited as she gathered her courage and her thoughts.

"Well." Zoe smiled and straightened her shoulders as though bracing herself. "I wasn't sure how to do this, so please forgive me if I'm stepping out of line or breaching protocol or something."

"You know you don't have to stand on formalities with me, Zo," Evan assured her and gave her hand an encouraging squeeze. "Go on. Just spit it out."

"Well, I've become close with someone I met through Brice. I can't tell you details about her, because that would be her story to share, or not, but I can tell you that she is a sub."

Evan made a 'come on' gesture with one hand and felt his shoulders relax. This was familiar territory for him. He was a Dom, so he was not surprised at the subject. To say he was relieved that this wasn't bad news concerning her or her husband, one of his closest friends, was an understatement.

"She approached me and Terryn about this almost a year ago now, and we've been coaching her and answering all her questions about the lifestyle."

"That's very nice of you girls. I couldn't think of more qualified teachers for her. She's a lucky girl." Evan smiled at the picture in his head of the two little subbies teaching this fledgling the ropes and preparing her for what was ahead. "Where do I come into this, sweetheart?"

"Okay." she braced her shoulders again and Evan was having a hard time keeping the smile off his face. She was so worked up over this, and so far she hadn't told him anything to cause this level of anxiety. "I need you to seduce her."

"Oh, there it is." Evan sat back in his chair in shock. Now he understood her nerves. "Zo, what the hell? Do you mean you want me to top her for a scene? Or take her on as my sub for a while?"

"No." She shook her head emphatically. "This would be easier if I could tell you everything, but I can't. The main problem is that she knows that she's a sub, but she's nervous. She's scared to try. Evan, she has been studying for *months* about this. She knows more than Terryn and I put together, but she won't do anything about it. She has been to the club as an observer only. Gage and I have scened for her on several occasions and Brice and Terryn, too. Brice and Terryn even invited her to join them to help her ease in to it, you know? So, she can experience it for herself with people she loves and trusts. But she won't. She gets right to the edge of saying yes and then she chickens out." Evan nodded, but he thought she was so caught up in what she was saying it wouldn't have mattered to her if he hadn't. "Well, you would think because she has gotten so close to Terryn lately that she would have at least said yes when she offered to let her come play with them, right? I thought for sure that would be the ticket, but no. Not even that." Zoe stared at him in frustration for a moment then concluded with, "So you see, it has to be seduction. Otherwise, she is never going to get out there. And she needs to, Evan. It's time, I know it is. She is ready."

"Zoe, pet." Evan shook his head at her. "I understand what brought you here, but this isn't the answer. You can't force someone to take this step. They have to make it when they decide *they* are ready, not when someone else thinks they are." He held up a hand when she opened her mouth in protest. "Now, listen. Hear me out. You know this type of relationship is all about open communication and trust. Those lines get crossed, and you got nothing but danger. Seduction doesn't have a hand to play in that game. Seduction is illusion and coaxing and subterfuge. The exact opposite of what a BDSM relationship stands for."

Zoe wasn't daunted. "How about if you just meet her? What if you came to her place tonight? She runs this great tavern, fantastic food, good music and a really warm atmosphere. It would be a perfect place for you two to meet, because since it's on her turf so to speak, she won't feel as vulnerable. Then, after you get to know each other and she sees how great you are, you can tell her you're a Dom and everything will be perfect." Zoe was so taken with the idea that she slapped her hands together and started to get up as though to leave.

"Whoa there, Zo." Evan chuckled and placed a restraining hand on her shoulder to keep her in her seat. "If you think that settles things, you got another think coming."

"Please, Evan. Please?" Her big blue eyes welled with tears and he felt his resolve crumble under the impact.

"Dammit." He ran a frustrated hand over his scalp. "I tell you what. I'll go to her place and meet her. But only if she knows I am coming, and she knows I'm a Dom. Understood?" Her quick nod wasn't convincing so he added, "I mean it. I refuse to ambush this girl, Zo. Besides, if this were to turn into something and she found out it started under false pretenses, it would demolish any chance we had at establishing trust between us. You know that."

"I know." Her sigh was full of defeat and frustration. "It's just so terrible to see her suffering."

"Suffering?"

She looked up in panic. "Oh, well, you know. Because she's a sub, but she's scared to leave the nest, you know?" Evan could tell she was backpedaling, but he let that go. She had told him more than once there was more to tell but that she was not at liberty to discuss it. He was intrigued and wanted to question her, but he knew that would be unfair, so he stood and helped her to her feet. "Text me the address and the time she'll be expecting me. I'll meet her, but I'm not making any guarantees. You've heard the old adage 'you can lead a horse to water but you can't make him drink'? Well, you can lead a sub to a whipping bench but you can't make them bend over it. She's going to have to make that choice all by her lonesome and there's nothing you or I can do about that."

"Of course." Zoe leaned in and hugged him tight for a second. "I didn't even think about the way it could have come across as a broken trust until you pointed it out. She'll know who and what you are before you even step foot in there, I promise."

Chapter Four

"He's not stepping foot in my place, Zoe!" Cami was horrified and not to mention mortified. "I can't believe you went to some stranger and told him I wanted him to come beat on me."

"Honey, you're overreacting a little, don't you think?" Ziporah rubbed soothingly on Cami's arm. "Zoe told you she didn't give your name or any details about you specifically. She is only trying to help."

"I know." Cami tried to pull the panic back in and think things through rationally. "You're right. I'm sorry I snapped at you, I just don't think I'm ready to take that step yet."

Cami heard both Zoe and Ziporah sigh over that and she cringed when Ziporah said, "Yes you are. It's time, Cam. It's time."

"Cam," Zoe said in a soft and gentle voice. "I've scened with Evan. He is the one and only Dom that Gage ever let touch me, so that says something, doesn't it?" Cami shrugged a little and Zoe went on. "He's freaking gorgeous, too, if that helps. Almost as tall as Gage, really great body, these amazing green eyes that just laser beam you and he's bald. Not bald in a creepy comb-over way. Bald in a– used to be a swimmer who was dedicated and fierce, oh my God he's freaking beautiful–way." Zoe tried a smile on her, but Cami was still reeling and wouldn't be charmed. When Ziporah laid her head on Cami's shoulder from behind, Cami reached back and cupped her hand on top of the other woman's silky hair. "I am just so scared of doing this alone. And of doing it at a club with a bunch of people watching, too. Why am I such a basket case? And how in the world is it possible for me to want something so much when it scares me this bad? This feels just like it did when you took me on my first roller coaster, Z. Remember how terrified I was?" When Z smiled and nodded, Cami added, "And then remember how you couldn't get me off the thing after you finally got me to try it? But, this is different, this is the biggest roller coaster in creation and I feel like I have to ride it all alone with no safety harness." She huffed in disgust at what she saw as her own shortcomings. "If only you were a sub, too. Then I wouldn't have to do this alone. We could do it together."

Ziporah stiffened and slowly straightened up. "I'm sorry. I shouldn't have said that. I'm being a baby."

"No. That's it." Ziporah looked as if she'd just been slapped, so Cami was unprepared for what she said next. "That's perfect. Why didn't we think of this before?"

"Wait a minute," Zoe said in a baffled voice, "you lost me."

"Me too," Cami said with a frown, puckering her brow.

"I'll do it with you!" Zoe's mouth popped shut and Cami could see her fighting to be polite. But this was her best friend and polite didn't factor for them, so Cami just burst out laughing right in her face.

"Hey!" Zip shoved her, but she did it with a good-natured chuckle. "Cut it out. Why not? I can be a sub with you."

"Zip, darlin', there isn't a submissive bone in your body," Cami told her, still laughing at the idea. "Especially with men. You chew them up and spit them out like sunflower seeds."

"I do not!" *Affronted.*

"Morgan Fisher." *Triumphant.*

"He was a chauvinist." *Disdainful.*

"Allen Brickman." *Smug.*

"Spineless." *Contemptuous.*

"Cary Griffin." *Challenging.*

"Fine." Ziporah threw her hands up in a huff and stomped to the coat tree in the entry way and, as she yanked on her black designer pea coat, she glared at Cami. "I can't believe you brought up Cary."

"I had to make you admit it. You could never be a sub. If anything, you'd be a Domme." Cami walked over and fussed with her friend's collar while she did up her buttons. "And, as much as I love you, Zip, I don't swing that way, so if you ever tried to whip me, all it would make me do is laugh." She softened the blow with a kiss to her friend's cheek.

"I know." Zip wasn't really mad; Cami could tell. "But, hear me out. It's just some kinky sex, right? Why can't I play with you for the first little while? It'll be exciting and crazy." She winked and Cami could tell the idea was really growing on her. "It'll be an adventure I can look back on someday. Something to tell all the other little old *bubbes* in the rest home to make 'em jealous when I'm in my eighties and sex is just a fond memory. Let me at least try. You never know, I might like it as much as you."

"What's a *bubbe*?" Zoe looked completely baffled.

"That's the Yiddish word for grandma," Cami answered Zoe with a small smile then looked to Z. Cami was absurdly touched. "You would really do this for me, Zip?"

Ziporah cupped both of Cami's cheeks in her palms and said, "You're my best friend. I would do anything for you."

Cami wavered. On the one hand, she knew that if Z were there doing this with her she wouldn't be so afraid to try. On the other ... "Z, BDSM is all about trust and honesty. You can't fake your way through this. It would be wrong. As much as I would love to have you there by my side, I can't let you do it."

"Oh, Cam." Ziporah rolled her eyes. "Give yourself a little break here and stop taking this all so damn seriously. I won't be faking, I'll be experimenting. I've been right here with you all along as you've dug into this lifestyle. Almost two whole years of books and websites and even that crazy seminar we schlepped our asses to.

"It sounds like a freakin' kick in the pants. This is a win-win situation for both of us. I'll get to try it out and let my freak-flag fly for a bit and you my dear, sweet, submissive friend, will get to ease into sexual awakening with your best friend there to hold your hand. Now, tell me, where is the wrong in that?"

Cami could find none, so she caved with a squeal and flung herself against Z in a bear hug. "Thank you! Oh-my-lanta this is going to be so crazy. I love you so much."

"I love you back. Now let me go, I have to stop by the precinct before I hit court, and if I hurry I can catch my idiot cousin before he breaks for lunch."

"Is that why you're running off right now? Z, he said he'd be there till one o'clock, you got another hour before you have to leave."

"Exactly," Z said with a smirk. "I gotta get there before he skips out early. Heck, it's what I'd do to him."

Chapter Five

"You are the stupidest man in existence. How in the world did you make detective? Did you sleep with the captain?" Ziporah inquired this of her cousin in a singsong voice, with a sugary smile on her face and her head tilted as though she were speaking to a toddler or a particularly oblivious puppy. She knew it would nettle him and make him wish they were still kids, so he could take a swing at her like he used to. It galled him that they were now too old to wrestle, and if she were honest, she had to admit that she missed it, too. Fighting with Brandon was just about the most fun she ever had, as a kid and as an adult.

"Zippy, my girl," he said, purposely using the nickname that drove her nuts. "Of course I slept my way to the top; you taught me everything I know about taking it up the ass."

It took all she had to keep from busting out a smile at that. Good one, she thought, but would die a fiery death before she would let him know.

"Ha-ha," she managed to say, without letting her true mirth show. "If you could just take your head out of yours and give me that file I requested, I can get to work trying to sew up all the holes you left in this case and send the bad guy to jail." She smiled in her best imitation of a great white shark just to needle him until he fished it out with some choice grumbling. Once she tucked it safely into her briefcase, she lost the snark and looked at him seriously. "Hey, can I ask a favor? I was hoping you could make it to Haven tonight for Cami and me. And please, bring Angie.

What she sees in you I'll never understand, but her presence makes yours bearable."

"Yeah, sure, even though you're going to be there. But, I guess putting up with you is the price I'll have to pay for hanging with Cami. Shame." He shook his head as though deeply saddened and Z had to again fight back a smile. He was on top of his game today. It was just like him to agree right off the bat, no questions asked.

"Good," she said as she gathered up her stuff so she could head out. "I think Brice and Terryn are going to be there already, but could you ask if Cade and Trevor will bring Riley?"

"Z," Brandon said, his voice suddenly solemn, "okay, you bet. But, should I be worried?" With a smile, she shook her head no. "We'll be there. I'll bring everyone I can. You guys got nothing to worry about."

The affection between them ran bone deep, and though in most cases they would rather choke than admit it–when it mattered, when it really and truly counted, they were there for each other.

"You know, sometimes, like now, I'm glad your mother didn't drown you in a river. I'm sure that will pass the next time you open your mouth, but for now, I am glad." The wink and grin he flashed her were more like his usual cocky self and she gave him her own grin in return before she turned and walked toward the door.

She was brought up short at the elevator when the doors slid open and two extremely handsome men walked out. One she knew.

Gage Hollister was a big Greek god of a man, with blond hair that was to die for and a body that made women weak in the knees. Although she liked him, she didn't know him well. She loved his wife Zoe though, and since he made her deliriously happy, Z was inclined to think the best of the big man. He was a close friend of her cousin's and she bumped into him at events like birthdays or similar gatherings, so she was slowly getting to know more and more of him. And each new thing she learned only endeared her to him more.

The man he was with was a stranger to her. And what a handsome one at that. Ziporah stood a little straighter and had a completely girl moment by frantically worrying if her lipstick was still in place, or if she had obliterated it with her coffee cup this morning.

He was tall, not as tall as his companion, but taller than her, so that was good enough. He was gorgeous. Green eyes that felt liked they were locked on her and one of those perfect masculine square jaw lines, that to her, spoke of strength of character. He had hints of dimples in his cheeks as well as his chin. He was also bald. She loved a strong, confident, bald man, and right now she was looking at the finest example of one that she had ever encountered.

"Well, hello there," Gage said in his panty-melting drawl. "It's been an age, Ziporah. How're ya?" He moved in for a warm brief hug. Z marveled that he would.

Ziporah had a reputation as a ballbuster. She worked hard to keep that intact. Her work brought her up against hardened criminals and smarmy defense lawyers every day. She had to be tough, smart and hard as nails to get where she was in her chosen career.

In spite of that, Gage never failed to treat her with that southern *Gone with the Wind* courtesy that made her feel feminine, fragile and cherished. She loved that about him.

Loved that he could treat her like a lady without making her appear or feel like he saw her as weak or beneath him. It was a rare man indeed who could pull that off.

"Ziporah." Gage swept out one hand toward his friend. "This is my good friend, Evan Grant. Evan, this here is Ziporah."

"Pleased to meet you," Evan said, and reached out to shake her hand.

"Likewise." Z barely managed to reply, not only was his hand warm, strong and giving her chills, she was mesmerized by his voice. The man had the same honey-dipped accent as Gage, only his was richer. Deeper somehow, and so smooth on the ears, she almost closed her eyes to savor it better. Just as she was about to draw away, the chips fell into place and shock sucker-punched her. This must be Master Evan.

"Holy shit."

"Excuse me, ma'am?" Ziporah felt a fire erupt in her cheeks. Crap, she hadn't meant to say that out loud.

"Oh, sorry," Z stammered as her brain frantically tried to come up with a plausible excuse. "I, uh, I just realized I forgot something important for my current case. Sorry."

"Where you rushin' off to, darlin'?" Gage asked. "We were just droppin' in to see if Brice and your cousin wanted to grab lunch. You got time to join in?"

"Yes, please do," Evan said. It hadn't escaped Z's notice that Evan hadn't taken his eyes off of her since he stepped off the elevator.

"Sorry guys," she replied, anxious to get away from his mesmerizing presence so she could think, "I have to be in court soon. Thanks, though. Have a good time."

Chapter Six

The rich, heavenly scent of cinnamon and apples filled the air of the tavern from the three pies cooling on the display rack, as well as from the three still in the back that should be coming out pretty soon. Cami polished the gleaming bar top with a clean rag, out of nerves rather than necessity. Everything that needed to be done for the night had been done.

The kitchen offered a decent number of choices. Cami paid top dollar for Natacha, the cook she had hired to insure the food would draw the people back just as much as the music and atmosphere. And boy was that ever the best decision she had made in her life. Not only was she amazing with her selection of meals, but the desserts the woman crafted were good enough to bring Cami to her knees.

"Here, try this." Natacha came out from the back, holding a spoon out for Cami.

"What is it?" The sauce in it was a bright pinky-orange.

"It's the guava sauce I made up for the cheesecake."

"Guava?" Hmm, Cami thought. That sounded scary. Cami didn't think she'd ever even tried a guava before, but Natacha hadn't steered her wrong yet. She opened up and the second the spoon hit her tongue, her knees turned to liquid.

"Oh. My. God." The Haitian cook giggled and delight filled her sparkling brown eyes as Cami slid down the bar and flopped her butt on the floor. "I can't believe this. Oh, wow. I wanna marry this sauce."

"I know, right?" Natacha joined her with a laugh and draped her arm along Cami's shoulders.

"No, seriously." Cami couldn't stop licking the spoon. The tangy-sweet-nothing ever tasted quite so good-flavor lingered on her taste buds like heaven. "I want to fill a pool with this and swim in it. I want to name my first child after it. I want–"

Natacha shoved her over and got up. "I get it, you like it." Cami stayed sprawled where she was and gazed up at her cook. She was a lovely curvy woman, with latte colored skin, a dash of freckles on her nose, full beautiful lips and natural hair. No weaves or straightening for this girl, she wore her hair loud and proud and was stunning in her god-given beauty. "I'm heading home. The cheesecake needs to cool for at least an hour, so no touching till I get back. You can have some tonight." She must have seen Cami shift her eyes toward the kitchen, because Cami got a swift kick on her hip. "I mean it, girl. You wait for tonight. I get back and see you've been poking in my kitchen, and you an' me's gonna have some words."

As she marched off toward the door, Cami called out, "You don't scare me!"

"Yes I do." Then the door shut with a swoosh and she was alone.

Cami pushed herself up and there was a smile of pure happiness on her face as she got back to work. The tension eased for a moment, thanks to her spunky friend.

An hour or so later, when slender tanned arms slipped around her from behind and she felt a familiar form press to her back, Cami let herself still for the first time all day.

"Everything looks amazing, Cam." Ziporah's voice soothed her raw nerves and brought a calm to her jittery stomach.

"I keep getting so nervous that I'm sure I'm going to puke, but since I haven't eaten today except for one tiny sip of heaven, I don't." She chuckled when she felt her friend shudder against her. Ziporah may have nerves of steel in a courtroom, but when it came to things she liked to call 'gross out boy stuff', she was a complete wimp. Puke was at the top of that list.

She let her head fall back on Z's shoulder and rested against her. It was the calmest she'd felt all day.

"I'm sorry that I'm such a basket case, Z." She huffed. "It seems like tonight is the most important night of my life. What if he doesn't like me?"

"Impossible."

What if I don't like him?"

"Again, impossible. Trust me on this one."

"What if you don't like him, or I'm not a submissive after all?"

"Cami." Z's voice was a soft caress. "Relax. Remember? This is an adventure. And you're not in it alone. In fact, I invited the whole gang here tonight, so we have plenty of back-up. If we don't like this guy, or things get off to a wrong start, there will be people we trust here, who happen to be in the know about this stuff, watching over us."

She turned around to rest her forehead against Z's and looped her hands around her neck. "I can't figure out why you haven't killed me in my sleep yet. Is it because you're having pity on me, or is it my fabulous cooking skills?"

Ziporah snorted at that, because they both knew she was the worst cook on the planet.

"You've been a beast." Ziporah kissed her on the tip of her nose and gave a quick squeeze before she turned to pour herself a cup of coffee and said, "But that's what besties are for. Remember when I was studying for the bar? I was so cranky, I was driving myself crazy. I don't know how you managed to put up with me." She cradled her coffee in both hands and leaned back on the counter. "This is payback." Then she smiled.

"Urgh," Cami groaned and hung her head, "please don't tell me I've been as bad as you were." Then she ducked away in the nick of time as Z took a swing at her.

Cami picked up a plate and served Z a slice of pie, the steam rising fragrant and mouthwatering. Since it smelled so good, she relented, with an inner scolding about how tight her jeans fit, and got herself a generous helping, too. She didn't dare go looking for the cheesecake until Natacha came back, because Natacha was right, Cami *was* afraid of her.

"C'mon," she said motioning with a nod in the direction of the table she wanted, "let's sit and eat this before my inner-Richard Simmons wakes up and catches me."

Chapter Seven

That night, Evan walked into Cami's tavern, Haven, with not one, but two women on his mind. One he was committed to meeting and possibly helping into the lifestyle, and the other he was hoping to get another chance at meeting someday. Ziporah had blasted him with her cool, commanding presence and had rocked him back on his heels. Quite a feat indeed, when less than an hour before, all he'd been able to think about was the coming meeting and its importance to someone he considered very dear. The two women had rooted into his brain and taken up permanent residency. He'd been useless for the rest of the day, distracted and unfocused on the work that had needed his attention.

But that was done. The endless afternoon was behind him now and he could set about getting to the mission at hand. Maybe someday, after Cami was settled into the role of sub and had either found a Dom or was comfortable enough to search for one on her own, he could find a way to get Ziporah's number from her cousin. Tonight, he was going to focus on the owner of this surprisingly welcoming establishment and see if he could help her determine if this was indeed the life for her.

Evan was planning on speaking with Cami, finding out how far she was willing to go and what she hoped to get from her time with him then possibly providing that service for her. Bondage, flogging, spankings and exerting his dominance, both verbally and physically in an effort to ease her into the world of BDSM, were the extent of his expectations. Now all he had to do was find out what hers were and see where that left them both.

As he made his way past the bar and toward the dance floor, the music was loud but not overly so, which was nice. He wouldn't have to shout to be heard, he liked that. The place was crowded. Since Zoe had given him some of the details about her and this place, he felt a measure of pride as he looked around. The woman was a lot more than a beauty with a stunning voice like he'd been told. She looked to have a hell of a head for business on her, too.

Evan spotted Gage easily. The man towered over everybody else there as he swirled his raven-haired wife around the dance floor with a grace and style that should be impossible for someone with his bulk. Just then, Gage dipped Zoe low and Evan saw a couple dancing right behind him. The sight froze him where he stood.

The two women who'd taken over his brain for the better part of his day were right there, dancing together. Ziporah had shed her suit jacket and power heels. She was dancing in her bare feet, wearing her snug grey skirt that ended a respectable two inches above her knees, and a plum colored camisole that left her long, toned arms as deliciously bare as her legs. She shimmied and swayed in perfect rhythm and Evan felt his palms itch with the need to touch.

The woman she was dancing with had to be Cami. Zoe had told him what she would be wearing and had given him a general description of her looks. He'd been told she was soft and curvy, with multi-hued blonde hair and a downright beautiful face. Well, it was a completely accurate description; yet at the same time not accurate at all. He stood where he was in stunned silence while he adjusted to the reality of the beauty that was her.

All those soft curves were bumping and grinding to the beat with a gusto that made him smile, even as lust tightened like a fist in his gut. She turned then, and when he got a look at her ass, all he could think was JLo had nothing on this woman. She dipped her knees and started pulsing and thrusting those jean-clad hips while she looked back over her shoulder with a saucy smirk for her friend, and Evan began walking without realizing it.

He wanted to have them both. It was a complication that they knew each other. Evan told himself that he had made a commitment to Zoe to see to her friend and that's exactly what he would do. The attraction he felt for Ziporah was just something he was going to have to lock away until he was free to pursue it.

Since Ziporah already knew him he came up behind her. "So, we meet again." She startled a little, but when she looked back and saw it was him, a dazzling smile lit up her face. He returned it and slid an arm across her waist to grab her opposite hand and spin her into a twirl with a flourish that even Gage would be proud of. She was laughing when he brought her back in to his side. He motioned with his chin toward Cami. "Introduce me to your friend." It wasn't a request. He was a Dom and it was a subtle way for him to test the waters to see how she would react to his authority; he said it with a smile to soften the command, but it was an order all the same. She smiled back and reached out just in time, as Cami had turned to leave. Ziporah towed her back with a yank.

"Cami," she said over the music, "this is Evan. He's the friend of Gage and the Marshall clan that Zoe told us about. Evan, this is Camille. Cami for short. My nearest and dearest."

He hadn't let go of Ziporah's hand, so he used his free one to reach out to shake Cami's. Like a switch had been flipped, the flirty buoyant attitude faded from Cami's eyes. Her smile didn't falter, but Evan caught the shift in her mood and that she took a tiny step in retreat. He noted as well that she whipped her free hand behind her back to keep away from the handshake he offered.

"Nice to meet you," she said with that bubbling smile still in place, even as he could actually see the lightness of her spirit fading away. "Welcome. I'm so glad you came. If you're a friend of Zoe's, the first drink is on the house and I'll even throw in a slice of pie."

She was panicky and ready to bolt. But she was a sexual submissive who had been researching for months about the lifestyle and what it meant to be what she was. He kept his hand out and said, "Cami, take my hand."

He felt a myriad of things when she bolstered her courage and shakily placed her hand in his.

The man in him was dazzled by her beauty. The Dom in him was challenged by her retreat. And the heart of him was wrenched by the vulnerability she was trying so hard to hide. In two short minutes, her fate was sealed. She would be his, he promised himself. Period.

Chapter Eight

Z could hardly believe Evan was here at last. She had been distracted by thoughts of him all afternoon. The judge had noticed, and it was so bad he'd asked her if she needed a recess to pull herself together.

There was just something so mouthwatering about him that she could not get him out of her thoughts. He had the same commanding air about him that Gage, Brice, Trevor and Cade all had. That presence that forced the attention of everyone around them. He wasn't for her though, she reminded herself. No matter what she said to Cami, the whole BDSM thing was not her cup of tea. No way. No matter how drool-worthy, nobody was her Master. But, as she let her gaze travel up and down the length of the gorgeous man in front of her, she couldn't help but wonder what it was going to be like to walk on the wild side with him. If ever there was a man who she would enjoy letting take control like that, she thought she just might be staring at him.

She didn't need or want more than that. It had taken her quite a while to realize that relationships didn't work for her. Her work came first, then Cami, and what energy she had left over didn't leave a lot of time for romance. Besides, she had found that men couldn't handle her no-nonsense approach, anyway. She was forward and abrupt and the few guys she had met who were turned on by that, for some reason, didn't turn her on.

Evan was still holding her hand, and the zings she felt zapping up her arm were giving her goose flesh. He winked at her, all slow and lazy, and Z swore she felt herself blush. God, she hoped he couldn't see it if she did. How embarrassing. She forced herself to look away so she could get a grip and caught the change in Cami. Shit.

Real Cami had gone bye-bye and fake Cami was smiling like a robot. Over the years, Cami had perfected hiding her emotions when things got too real for her. She could put up a front and be nothing but sunshine and roses, even while inside, her world was crumbling. For Cami to be doing this now meant only one thing – she was attracted to Evan. Nothing scared that woman more than a man she thought was sexy. So on one hand, this was perfect. On the other, it was going to be a battle for her friend. Cami had to face that fear and climb over it like a hurdle in order to then climb the next one, which was taking her first steps into a world that scared her almost as much as it intrigued her.

Z knew that Zoe hadn't told Evan about the change in plans, so he wasn't expecting her to join their party. They would find a way to break it to him later tonight. For now, Cami came first. She always had since they first met. Even before that terrible night, Z had felt a protective connection to her. After that night, it had only gotten stronger. If this guy affected Cami so much from just meeting him, Z knew that this was the right choice for them. The right choice for Cami especially.

So she made a snap decision. She was still holding both of their hands and gave them each a squeeze. "Hey! I gotta hit the restroom. Evan, will you dance with Cami while I'm gone? Thanks."

She told herself that she wasn't abandoning her best friend. She was merely acting like a mother bird and kicking her from the nest so she would be forced to spread her wings and fly. If Cami was in fact a sub, and she liked this guy as much as Z thought she did, then Z couldn't think of a better way for her to find out or a better time to start.

Z felt no guilt whatsoever about ducking out when Cami was scared. Dr. West had said that it was time for Cami to face those fears and take back what had been stolen from her. It was past time. Besides, her cousin the cop was dancing right behind her and there was another cop, plus three really big and scary guys, here tonight that would happily rip Evan's arms off if he got out of line. That was why she had invited them all here in the first place.

"Don't go." The order was not unexpected. Who it came from, however, was. Evan leaned in and whispered in her ear, "Your friend has frozen up like a popsicle. You leave now, and I guarantee she'll bolt like a rabbit."

"How can you …?" Z was shocked. Cami was still smiling with serene politeness and gave every outward appearance that all was well in her world. It had taken Z ages to recognize when Cami did this. How in the hell did he see it when he'd never even met her before? Z looked at Even in a new light and not a small amount of awe. In her experience, men just weren't this observant or considerate. Ziporah made a mental note to buy Zoe flowers. The girl had picked out the perfect Dom.

"It's in the eyes," he said, and turned to smile gently at Cami. Yeah, it is, Z thought. Only how did he see it?

"Well, you're a big, strong boy." Z leaned close to him and taunted, with her lips brushing his ear as she spoke. "Don't let her." Then she sailed away with so much swing in her saunter she nearly threw her back out.

Her exit was ruined however, when her cousin caught up to her just as she rounded the bar. "Hold up there, Zip. What was that?" Much in the same way she had done with Cami, Brandon yanked her by the arm and turned her to face him.

"What are you talking about?" Z tried to keep a cool and unaffected expression on her face. It wouldn't do to let her overbearing and protective cousin see she was upset and jittery over the possibilities turning in her head. He loved to see her coming apart at the seams, but only as long as he was the one holding the seam ripper. Anybody else upset her and he turned into a beast.

"I'm just going to the bathroom detective, sheesh." She tried to keep her voice nonchalant instead of touched; nobody in the world loved her quite the way this man did. "Am I breaking some law that I'm not aware of?"

"Cut the shit for once, Z." Brandon was all seriousness and just his expression alone let her know he wasn't fooled. Didn't mean she was going to make it easy for him. "What? Let me go. I have to pee."

"There are so many things going on right now I don't know where to start. Are you really going to be petty enough to make me list them?" He ground his teeth so hard she was surprised they didn't crack when her answer to that was nothing but stony silence and a raised eyebrow.

"Okay, be a bitch about it then." With a growl he tugged her to the hall where the music was muted and the only people around were the ones headed in and out of the bathrooms. Then he backed her up to a wall and started ranting in a low enough volume that only she could hear.

"First off, I wanna know how you got on fucking Evan's radar. That guy is dangerous, Zip. He's into crazy shit I'm not going to tell you about, but I don't like the way you lit up when he was talking to you.

"Second. What the fuck? Some guy–forget who at the moment–lights you up like that, and you pass him off to Cami?

"And that leads to three. Why in hell are you handing Cami off to a guy? Which brings this trip through Wonder-fucking-land back to the first problem: Evan God Damn Grant?"

Ziporah was speechless. "That's a lot to pick up on from watching two minutes on the dance floor."

"I'm a cop. Observant is a job requirement."

"Now I'm the one who doesn't know where to start." She ran her unsteady hands through her hair and tried to bring order to her thoughts. "Cami." Of course, as always, her first thoughts were of her friend. "Cami is fine. You and three other big strong men are out there. That's why I asked you all to come in the first place. Plus it's only a dance or two. Nothing is going to happen in the middle of her bar and I highly doubt a man Gage Hollister introduced me to is going to try anything shady, anyway." She reached out and put a comforting hand over his heart. "Cami likes him. I could tell the minute she looked at him that she does. Bran, she hasn't liked somebody in forever, it won't hurt to see if maybe this can go somewhere." She smiled and tried to lighten the mood. "Even if that somewhere is just to bed. If anybody on this planet needs to get laid good and proper, it's Cami."

"But, Zip." Brandon got that tender tone in his voice that he only got when he was being very careful with her and every time he did, it made her cry. "You like him, too. Don't give me that look, and close your mouth. I saw your face when he touched you and I saw the look on your face when you decided to pass him off." His big calloused palm cupped her hand where it still rested on his heart and he said, "I know you and Cami have a bond. We all love her. But, you gotta stop putting your life on the back burner for her. She's your best friend, but you have got to stop being Maryann to her Ginger. Sweetheart, didn't anybody ever tell you? *You're supposed to be the leading lady in your own life, cuz.*"

Absurdly touched, Z felt tears clog her throat. "Gilligan's Island? Really? I swear you stopped growing at twelve." She pulled him in for a tight hug. Then sniffed and said, "Now, for God's sake, stop watching Nick at Night before Angie finds out and leaves you for a real man."

"She watches it with me. She loves Lucy." His grin was as idiotic as his taste in entertainment.

"Urgh," she scoffed, "you guys *are* perfect for each other."

"Now," she continued, "I love that you are concerned. I know what you are trying to say, but you are worried for nothing. Cami and I are great. I'm not taking a back seat, really. This is just a guy, Brandon. He could be any guy, it's just like I'm passing up on a dress we both like or a pair of shoes–or wait–not shoes." She winked at him. "I'd gladly strangle her if the right shoes were on the line. In fact, we'd probably fight to the death over that."

"I'm calling bullshit on that. I know you." He took a breath and added, "I'll let that go though. You've been her mother hen for so long now; no way am I going to make you see it standing in a bar for a five-minute chat. Let's talk about this 'just a guy' then. I don't like either of you tangling with him."

"Brandon." Ziporah dropped her hands and stood tall to give him her best lawyer look. "On that point, I'm going to tell you it's none of your business who either Cami or I date. You have always tried to stick your nose in when it comes to who we date, but this is not the Victorian era and we are not your chattel. The both of us can make those choices for ourselves."

"I know." Brandon gave her his best bad-cop expression and crossed his arms over his chest. "And you've both told me to fuck off every time I've tried to step in. I'd like to point out that neither of you stuck with any of the jerk-off's I hated, so that should speak to my record. And this guy is different, Z. He's into kinky shit like Brice."

"I kind of figured that out for myself, even without being a big scary detective."

"Smartass. So, you know what he is. But do you know what it means to be what he is? Do you know even half of what it is to be into that? I do."

Shock snapped her mouth shut at that. How did her no-nonsense, raised in the 'burbs cousin, come by this knowledge?

"Brice is so fucking into it, he made it seem amazing and hot. So I tried it a couple years ago. Fucking crazy ass shit, Z. Crazy. I am talking tied-up and hanging from the ceiling while a guy, or two or three, whips and canes you and then fucks you in every hole you got. No way are you going to tell me you or Cami are into that. No fucking way."

"No," Z said as the mental picture that put in her mind caught and stayed. Much to her shock, not in a bad way, either. "No, I'm not telling you anything. My sexual preferences are my own damn business. And if I decide I want to see what all the fuss is about, that's my choice, not yours. And the same goes for Cami. Besides, for now, this is just a dance. Just be here and be supportive, okay? Look, this is her business, but I know you won't let it go otherwise, so well, Cami has been looking into the possibility that she is a submissive. If he likes her enough, he is going to help ease her in. And, I am, too."

"What the hell, Z! That's why you wanted us all here?" He looked as if she'd just sucker-punched him while he processed that. "Wow, I didn't see that coming. I'm supposed to be okay with that? Fuck me. No, close your smartass mouth. I know. I know it's not my place, you're grown women and able to make your own choices and all. Just gimme a minute, okay?"

Ziporah watched as the caveman part of his nature struggled with the reasonable part and she almost felt sorry for him. He was a strong alpha-male and he saw it as his duty to watch over those he deemed as his, and when his charges bucked his rule, it was always a battle for him to rein it in and let them be. "You and her are both going to go there, hmm? You? A sexual submissive? That's all well and good I guess. I still don't like it. By the way, there is no 'if he likes her'. He's in, Z. I saw his face when he looked at her. He's in." As the import of that sank in, Brandon added, "Just so you know, I was watching him with you both. And he's not only all-in on Cami, Z; he's all-in on you, too."

Chapter Nine

She left me … She left me … I can't believe she left me. The shocking mantra ran in a loop through Cami's brain, as she outwardly smiled and swayed to the beat. She fought back the urge to laugh as she flashed on a scene from Jurassic Park where the jerk lawyer left the kids to face the T-Rex alone. In this scenario, that scene was apt, because she felt as small and defenseless as those little kids facing the man in front of her. His gaze was like a tractor beam and never left her face. And the look in that gaze was decidedly ravenous.

The music was upbeat and lively with a sexy undertone that the people around her were picking up on as their dancing got more and more risqué. Her partner had some good moves on him. He danced close, keeping her pelvis tight to his as he dipped and pulsed in perfect rhythm, with a firm one-handed grip on her hip. He weaved her through the other dancers as though they weren't even there and Cami barely felt her feet touch the floor.

If she got any more attracted to this guy, she would probably combust.

For what seemed like the dozenth time, Cami tried to smile and extract herself from his hold and failed. It wasn't that she felt he was *making* her stay, because that would scare her and close her down, it was more like he was making her not want to go. She didn't know how he was doing it, but it was freaking her out. And if she were being honest, turning her on, too. And *that* was freaking her out as well. If this is what it felt like to be a sub, she was in trouble.

"You got so much going on in your pretty head, I'm surprised there isn't steam coming out of your ears." Oh God. He had a southern drawl. It was light but unmistakable, and Cami felt her knees turn to jelly. She loved a man with an accent. He'd come in even closer to speak directly into her ear and then, with a jolt, Cami realized he was staying there. The hand on her hip slid up and around to press between her shoulder blades, and now she felt every inch of him from breast to knees. Speaking of knees, with the next step he smoothly inserted one of his between hers and rocked their bodies with a pulsing grace that was primal.

She would have felt trapped and claustrophobic if not for the fact that he left his other hand free at his side. It was like he knew she was ready to bolt if he pushed her too far, so he left an escape hatch open for her in order to help her keep the panic at bay.

"Sorry," she finally remembered to respond. "I'm just distracted. It's busy tonight and I'm worried I don't have enough people on staff. It's a lot to think about, running a business."

"I bet." There was something in his eyes that told her he wasn't buying work as her excuse, but he didn't comment. "It's a fantastic place. You should be proud."

"I am." As warmth seeped into her from the large hand holding her so securely in the middle of her back, Cami finally found the presence of mind to move. "And I should get back to check on things now." Easing through the escape hatch he provided, she half expected him to try and stop her, considering how tight his grip was. But he didn't. So, of course, as soon as she was free, she wished she could step back in.

It was a little surprising. This was her standard boyfriend material test, and he had just passed. Whenever she danced with a man she was considering dating, she always broke off before the end of a song. Although she never put it into words, even to herself, she tested them to see who would let her go when she wanted.

Not too many had passed. And she did not expect a Dom to be one of the few who did. Weren't they supposed to be first in line in the control department? Also, most of the men who did agree to stop before the end of the song usually tried to follow her, but not this one. He stood in the middle of the floor where she left him and just watched her walk away with a fire in his eyes that made her want to turn around and march right back to him.

She was in trouble. But it was the kind of trouble she thought she just might finally be ready for.

Chapter Ten

An hour later she was helping bus some tables since the two girls on tonight were getting run ragged. *Note to self: hire more waitresses.* Maybe she'd see if Angie wanted to pick up some extra shifts.

Evan had spent most of that time at the pool tables with Brice and the other Doms. She had felt the intensity of his regard the whole time, though. It was like his stare had a gravitational pull and she was drawn by it. It was as exciting as it was terrifying.

"Sing for me." Ziporah snagged the tray from her hands. "I'll take over helping if you sing." Cami bit her lip and looked around. The place was packed and the energy was upbeat with just a touch of sultry to it.

"Okay," she told her, "but let's sing together. What better way to let him know we come as a set and show him exactly what he's getting himself into? And only if we can sing *Black Velvet*." She laughed when Z dropped her head back with a groan.

"Why do you hate me so much, when all I want is to love you?" Laughing outright, Cami took hold of Z's hand and led them to the stage.

"Come on. Let's play like we used to and see if we can light a fire in him." Cami's giggle was full of mischief.

"Why, Camille! I'm shocked." Z mocked her in a snooty drawl that only made Cami laugh harder.

Black Velvet had been their favorite song in college. For Cami it still was, but Z had decided that she was done with it after singing it a million and one times. Z didn't have the passion for music that Cami did, but she had a fantastic voice and Cami was convinced that Z could have been a rock star if she wasn't so bent on the law.

Once they hit the stage, Cami signaled to one of the bartenders and the lights dimmed until the two of them were spotlighted. She grabbed her guitar from its stand and used the control panel at her feet to turn on the mic. She was going to go acoustic, so she angled a second mic to catch the instrument and then handed a third to Z.

Cami wasn't big on speeches or rambling on before a song unless she needed to get the crowd's attention. Since this crowd had already given them their attention as soon as the lights dimmed, she just strummed the strings and started singing. "Mississippi in the middle of a dry spell ..." The lyrics flowed out like warm molasses, sexy and haunting. There were some songs that just hit her vocal abilities in their sweet spot, and this was one of them.

On stage, she wasn't shy. She wasn't a small town girl whose hips were too big. And most importantly, she wasn't that girl who'd been attacked. On stage, she was a completely different person and everything melted away but the music. Back in college it was what had saved her sanity.

As she sang, she knew she was killing it. Each note perfect and crystal clear, and the audience knew it, too. She had them eating out of the palm of her hand before she got to the first chorus. When the chorus did come, and Z chimed in with her precision harmony, it was like the stars had aligned and Cami wished she could freeze this one perfect moment in time, because it just didn't get better than this to her way of thinking.

She winked at Z because she knew that her friend felt the charge in the air too, and then looked out over the crowd to include them in on the magical moment, and that's when she saw him.

Almost like he had his own spotlight, Evan stood out from the crowd like a beacon. As soon as her eyes met his, he stood from the table and made his way across the packed room as though it were empty. He moved so fluidly it seemed as though he were floating, but that wasn't the right word for it. He moved too purposefully, too aggressively to call it floating, she thought. He was like a stalking animal, all muscle and strength, moving like water wrapped in a skin of stunning beauty.

The audience melted away until it was the three of them, alone in the universe. As the sultry song poured from them like verbal crack, Evan stood at the front of the stage and devoured every note.

Z and she always danced suggestively when they sang this one, but they had done so tongue-in-cheek and made it playful rather than uber-sexy. This time there was nothing playful about it. With Evan watching, every touch and shimmy and arch was a promise and a tease, and Cami had never been so turned on in her life.

All the men she'd been with since college had been attractive to her on some level, and she got excited plenty. She was working hard to take back her sexuality and despite what Z and her therapist believed, she was not content with the way things were. She had done her research and she had gotten very close to Zoe and Terryn, who had been a tremendous help in her quest of self-discovery.

EMBRACING THE FALL

She wanted more than anything to experience passion; she was ready for this. Ready for him. And even though it scared her to be this attracted to a man because it triggered bad memories, she wanted more than anything to take him up on the promises his eyes were making right now. With Z at her side, the fear of what was to come later was fading and in its place was the passion that she dreamed of.

Z stepped close and the two of them started crooning into the same microphone, cheeks brushing and breaths mingling. Cami knew the image the two of them made, with both their mouths so close to the bulbous head of the mic. And when Z trailed her fingers teasingly along it, she knew that it was a deliberate taunt to the man standing in front of them. She watched as the skin on his face tightened with arousal and his fists opened and closed at his sides like he was fighting to keep from reaching out and grabbing them.

Alone, that would frighten her, but tonight she wasn't alone and she felt no fear at all, only intense pleasure and a sense of free-falling adventure. She snuck a peek over to where Cade, Trevor and Riley were dancing. The three of them had been together for years now and looked happier than almost any couple Cami had ever known. They had two adorable children and the men couldn't keep their hands off of the woman they had taken as wife. If they could make it work so beautifully long term, surely the three of them could make a go of it too, even if it was just for the short term. Looking back at Evan and the look of undisguised desire she plainly saw on his face, yeah, she thought, she was more than ready to take this leap.

"Another." Evan was so turned on right now, he felt savage with it. The two women had just finished their song and the crowd around him was going ballistic. Cheers and catcalls and applause so abundant, it sounded like it was coming from an audience three times its size as it thundered around him. But that was all on the peripheral. Right now it was just the three of them, caught up in a force-field of energy that was blocking out the rest of the world and binding them together irrevocably.

"Again," he repeated, though he knew they had heard him. They both had their eyes riveted on him as though he was their Master and this was a scene.

They looked to each other and a silent signal was passed. They took way too long for his liking to bow and thank the others, and then more lights went on over the stage as Cami touched her foot to more controls. They moved the stands out of the way and just held the microphones by hand. Cami put her guitar to the side and brought up the music with some more foot-activated controls.

Sexy and slow was replaced with holy-fucking-hell-I'm going-to-combust-right-here hotness when the two of them put their amazing voices to *Take Me or Leave Me* from the Broadway show Rent, and the crowd lost its ever loving mind.

They taunted and pressed their bodies against each other while they sang with voices that slid into his ears, wrapped around his heart, grabbed him by his cock and refused to let go. It was the most turned on he ever remembered being while still fully clothed. They were pure sexual challenge up there, and the Dom in him was more than ready to accept that challenge. He didn't know how he was going to make this work but, somehow he was going to make them both his.

Cami was completely confident on stage. Gone were the shadows that had haunted her eyes while they danced. Instead she was bold and flirtatious; grinding against Ziporah like they were lovers and stirring the audience into a fevered pitch of frenzy as she dropped to her knees and dared the other woman to deny her appeal.

In contrast, Z was less confident than she was off stage. Gone was her kick-ass and take-no-shit persona, and in its place was a beautiful woman who was soft and approachable. She was saucy instead of defiant, and bubbling with laughter instead of bristling with challenge. She wasn't a hardened lawyer always on guard up there, but a woman with no barriers and no walls.

He was supposed to be here for Cami, but looking at them together, he found himself impossibly drawn to both women. *Equally*. Looking at them and trying to choose felt as though he would have to pick between either is right eye or his left. *Impossible*.

He hadn't a clue on how he was going to resolve that. He only knew if he didn't get his hands on them both soon, he was going to go insane.

Chapter Eleven

Two a.m. rolled around and the exodus from the tavern was slow and loud. Nobody was ready to leave yet as the food, drink and entertainment had all been equally top notch. Cami had opened the stage for the remainder of the evening and she cleverly steered away from the drunken or obnoxious and chose people who were actually talented to take a turn at singing. The result had created an atmosphere that was electrified and buoyant. It wasn't a wonder no one wanted to leave. He was right there with them.

To keep himself from dragging the women out of the tavern caveman-style, Evan chose to help with the after-hours clean up.

As he stacked chairs, his focus never wavered from where the two women were. It had been like that all night and had only grown in intensity after their time on stage.

When he had hit the pool tables for a round of doubles with Brice, Cade and Trevor, he knew their exact location the whole time. It was as if they were already his and they were seared on his consciousness irrevocably.

Now, as he took his time aligning the tables while the others were finishing up and saying their goodbyes, he tried to rein himself in. These ladies were not part of the BDSM world yet, and the last thing he wanted to do was scare them off before he'd even gotten started.

"You got yourself a long road ahead of you there, friend." Gage's soft drawl brought Evan's head around and he met the others man's stare straight on.

"Yes, it appears that way. So I take it Zoe talked to you about our visit this morning?" Evan asked as he crossed his arms over his chest and leaned against the table.

"Yeah, she did." Gage crossed his own arms over his massive chest and spread his stance like he was on the deck of a ship, and Evan had to fight from rolling his eyes. Gage was in lecture mode. "Have you spoken with Zoe or either of them tonight? I mean about the fact that it's gonna be both of them now, not just Cami?"

Evan almost fell over from shock. "So, that was what that duet was all about? How come Zoe didn't mention that this morning?"

"Seems Cami is so scared of movin' things forward that she was refusing to even meet with you. Then Ziporah stepped up and offered to try it out with her." Evan was torn. It was exactly what he wanted, however … "This isn't something to be taken lightly. I'm not a dabbler and I won't scene with someone who is."

"No. I know you wouldn't." Gage looked him in the eye for a moment then said, "I have gotten to know Ziporah over these last couple years. When Zoe told me what the two had planned, she expected me to blow my top and put a stop to the whole thing. I didn't though. You know why? Because I think that girl is a sub under all her prickly bravado." Gage smiled softly and watched as the lady in question was currently having a heated debate with her cousin. "She likes to think she's invincible, but there are times I look at her and I swear a good wind would break her into a million little pieces. That's why, when Zoe told me that she wanted to sub with Cami as a favor, I was all for it. I think that woman is every bit a sub just like her friend. But, there is something else troubling me." Gage seemed to be choosing his words carefully, so Evan stayed quiet and let him continue without interruption. "You're a good man and an even better Dom, Evan. You wouldn't push those girls where they can't go, so I know they're in good hands. It's you I'm worried about."

Nothing could have shocked Evan more, and if he hadn't already been half sitting on the table, he would've been knocked to the floor by that.

"What is that supposed to mean?" he asked, truly baffled.

"I know the kind of Dom you are." Gage leaned forward, like he needed to make sure Evan was hearing him. "I've never met a Dom more adept at bringing the dark to the light for a sub. You have a gift for opening them up during a session so nothing is hidden. But, these two are special. I don't know details; still, I know enough. And it's both of them. They got some serious trauma buried between them. What happens if you play this wrong and trip on a land mine?" They both looked to where the women in question burst into laughter with Zoe and a couple of the others. "Evan, you strip yourself emotionally bare when you go into a scene like no Dom I've ever known; it's like you're walking onto a battle field naked. And these two? They could damn well blow you up."

For a moment Evan was quiet as he let what Gage said sink in. Then he shook himself out of it and shoved him out of the way as he got back to picking up the chairs. "You damn mother hen. I know you mean well, but it's out of my hands at this point." With a shrug, he lifted his palms up in a gesture of helplessness. "They're already mine, Gage. I had already decided that I was going to have Ziporah before you mentioned anything, so you see? They are already mine. Now, go cluck over your sub and leave me alone." He knew Gage meant well. But seriously? Worried about *him?* He was a Dom and it was his job to look after the women who agreed to be his subs. That was a level of trust every Dom had the fucking responsibility to nurture.

Yeah, he maybe sometimes went a little too deep. And perhaps he took on their pain more often than not. For him, that was a price he was willing and, if he really looked at it, honored to pay.

BDSM done right was just as much–if not more–in the head as it was in the flesh. A sub had to open up their very soul in order to let a Dom find who they really were inside and bring their true nature and desires into the open. By god, if they were going to put that much faith in him, he wasn't going to come into this with anything less than all that he was.

The others were saying their goodbyes and filing out, and he was just putting the last of the chairs up on the last table when Cami surprised him by walking straight up to him. He would have guessed it would be Ziporah who would be the one to make the bold move, not Cami. But there she stood, shoulders back and a brave smile on her lovely face.

Most of her make-up had melted away, leaving her skin pale and dewy. Those luscious lips had just the faintest trace of red paint still on them and her eyeliner was smudged. As he waited to hear what she had to say, he wondered if this was how she would look after sex. Damp and a little wilted; it was sexy as hell.

"So, umm, Zoe said her and Gage would stay and Terryn said the same about her and Brice. But, umm, see my friend

Z?" She fidgeted where she stood and her feet pointed toward each other as she waived one hand in the general direction of her friend.

Evan took pity on her. "I already spoke with Gage. I know that Ziporah is interested in joining us." He smiled gently at her and placed a hand on her shoulder to soothe.

"And that's okay with you?" she asked, wide eyed.

"I'm looking forward to it." He nodded.

Her shoulders wilted in relief so drastically it was comical. "That's wonderful. Thank god." She started fidgeting again and said in a rush, "So, I guess the next step is safe words and limits. I know I don't want any blood play or anything with urine–gross, and–" Evan chuckled and placed one finger on her trembling lips. "You know, this isn't a typical situation. This also isn't a club setting and this is going to be the first BDSM experience for the both of you, right?" At her timid nod he continued. "Why don't we do it this way? Let's take some time to get to know each other a little first. How does that sound?"

"That sounds wonderful actually. Hey! I know. We could go to our place and have a Buffy-thon and drink till we can't walk straight. Would you like that?" She gave him wide hopeful eyes and chewed on her bottom lip.

That was a loaded question if he ever heard one. Evan tore his gaze up from where she was biting her bottom lip and looked her right in the eyes.

"What the hell is a Buffy-thon?"

Her laugh was infectious and tugged a reluctant grin from him, which was no small feat considering how aroused he'd been all night.

"Buffy, The Vampire Slayer," she managed to get out after a few moments. "It's only the best cult classic show of the ninety's. Really. Clever, funny as heck and addicting. Didn't you watch it back then?"

Evan fought to keep the laugh locked behind his lips. He was sure that was not meant to be a joke. "No, sweetheart, I did not. In fact, I've never even heard of it."

"Oh my gosh! Then you *have* to come. Because seriously, even though it was written for teenage girls, this show is awesome. The creator, Joss Whedon, is a sci-fi god."

"Well, we'll have to see about that." He slipped his hand up to cup the back of her neck and enjoyed watching her flush in reaction to his touch. "Does Ziporah know you're inviting me?"

She had to swallow before she could answer, a fact he noted with pleasure. "She will when you get there."

In that moment, Evan saw that he had a brat on his hands. "Perfect. Put your address and number in my phone and I'll be right behind you two."

She gave a happy bounce and a squeal, and then rocked back and forth on her heels as she typed in his phone. He was studying her bent head as she did, then she floored him with her whispered words. "I know that Zoe and Terryn probably told you I'm a chicken. But, I'm ready for this. I want this and I'm really happy that they picked you."

He nodded first and took a moment before he spoke, not trusting his voice right away. "That's lovely to hear, sweetheart. I'm really glad they picked me, too."

"Mm-hmm," she swallowed again and licked her lips. After she handed his phone back, she lifted her face before she added, "I'm not scared." And walked away.

The hell she wasn't, he thought. The fact that she was and wanted to face those fears about brought him to his knees. He grabbed his coat from a table and headed for the door; life just got a hell of a lot more interesting.

Chapter Twelve

"You did what?" Ziporah could not believe what she had heard. "Repeat that, please, because I know you did not just say that you invited Evan over."

"Yes, my friend I did just say that." When Cami tried to bounce away like it was no big deal, Z grabbed her by the hand.

"Hey," she said in a voice soft but stern. "We were just supposed to meet him tonight. You know, see if we liked him and then go from there."

"Well, we did like him. I know you liked him as much as I did. And he's not coming over to tie us up. He's coming to watch Buffy with us. Just to get to know us better. That's all."

"Oh, all right, I guess. I still can't believe we are doing this." A quick kiss to her temple and then she went on. "Millions of people are into it, but it feels so weird to think that if everything goes right, we are going to be letting this man put us in shackles and spank us."

"Z? You don't think I'm like this because of what happened to me, do you? Or that it happened because I'm like this?" Her voice was small and it was tinged with the guilt and shame that a lot of survivors carried. Z cursed quietly, yet with venom, as she pulled Cami into a fierce hug.

"Of course not, idiot. You have asked yourself those same questions over and over again. And every time, you get the same answer. You were a submissive long before that happened to you, and you don't stop being who you are just because you were attacked. And you were attacked because of who he was–an asshole–not because of anything that had to do with who you are."

Cami smiled and said, "Okay. You're right. I know. Just god! I'm so mixed up. What if–"

"Relax," Z murmured and moved away to make some popcorn. "I'm going to be right here the whole time. No use torturing yourself with what ifs. Let's just strap in and enjoy the ride."

"Hi," Cami thought her voice sounded like the squeak of a teenage boy in puberty and tried not to grimace as she faced Evan at the door. "Come on in." She stepped back and motioned him ahead of her. "Can I get you a drink? We got just about everything and non-alcoholic stuff too, if you are done drinking for the night."

As he shrugged out of his jacket and handed it to her, Cami almost moaned. Not only was it leather, but it was soft as butter and smelled deliciously of him. It brought back all of the tingling feelings she'd had every time he got within range of her this evening.

She followed him through the short hallway into their living space. Z could afford a place on her own, barely, and so could Cami, but in those cases with the cost of living in New York City, they would be dismal places indeed. But together, they were able to afford an apartment that was spacious, above ground and in an area that they both felt safe walking home to.

As Evan looked around, Cami felt pride in her and Z's home. It was lovingly decorated by both of them, with

Cami's country living touches finding harmony with Z's more sleek modern style.

"Nice place you girls got here." Evan's warm voice filled the room and Cami almost closed her eyes to savor the rich tone of it.

"Thanks." She tugged a bright colorful throw blanket out of the way and motioned him toward the couch. "This is the prime TV seat. Z and I fight over it all the time. So, as honored guest, you get to sit here."

The smile he shot her was hot enough to melt snow and Cami caught herself sighing as she snuggled the blanket into her chest. Fire erupted in her cheeks when she heard him chuckle because he caught her, too. "Umm, here." She flung the blanket at him and headed into the kitchen. "I'm gonna see if Z needs help with the snacks. What would you like to drink?"

"Whatever you two are having is fine with me," Cami heard as she almost tripped in her haste to flee.

"Oh my God, Z." She was breathless and scared and more excited than she remembered being in a long time. "He's so hot. And his voice! Did you hear him? That accent turns my legs to jelly, I swear."

"Yeah," Z said as she loaded up the pretty serving tray they found at a craft fair in Central Park last spring. "It's enough to make any girl turn to jelly, so don't feel too bad."

"Hey, Evan?" Cami called out, "we are going to be just a minute, okay?"

"No problem, ladies," he replied, "take your time."

"What's up?" Z asked, still staring at the tray like it held the answers to the mysteries of the universe. "Why did you do that?"

"So you can tell me what's wrong." Cami inched closer and rested her forehead on Z's. "Spill it, sweetie. Two minutes ago you were all no-nonsense and take charge, and now you look like a good wind could knock you down. Is it Evan? Want me to ask him to go? I will. We don't have to do this if you don't want to. I can do it on my own. I'm a big girl, I'll be fine." Cami reached up and stroked one hand over the chic glossy bob of Z's dark hair. It was like running her hand over satin; it was so smooth and healthy.

The fact that Z didn't move or immediately shoot down her concerns had Cami worried. Z was the strong confident one between the two, so if she was afraid to speak up, something must be terribly wrong.

"Don't ask him to leave," she finally whispered, and with a sigh, turned to wrap one arm around Cami's waist and place one hand lovingly on her cheek. "But, I didn't expect this, Cam. I like him, too. A lot. It's making this seem more important than I thought it would be."

Cami saw the same expression on Z's face whenever she was telling her a hard truth, like when her bird had flown away because Z had forgot to close the window. Or when Z told her their friend Angie had been attacked and that they didn't know if she was going to make it.

So, seeing that same look now told Cami that she had better think before she spoke. Evan was handsome, no doubt. But, they had just met him today and Z wasn't the type to get all girly over a boy. For her to confess this now meant that Z must be as nervous about this next step as Cami was herself. Somehow, that was more encouraging to Cami than all of the coaching she'd been getting so far. If her stalwart and unflappable Ziporah was all flustered and excited too, then that meant that she wasn't alone.

So, in the spirit of solidarity, she wrapped an arm around Z's tense shoulders and said, "Okay. So what?" With a cheeky smile that she always used to get Z to give in to her, she grabbed the serving tray. "It's a Buffy-thon. Then who knows? We're here to explore, right? To embrace our fantasies and desires? Open ourselves up to that lifestyle and you to the adventure of a lifetime? Let's go out there and face this. Together, like we've faced everything." She laughed like a loon at the jaw-dropped look Z gave her. "What? You're the only one who can be encouraging and strong? I'm not allowed to give you a boost when you need it?"

"Well, no," Z said in a mock stern voice as she tried not to smile and failed. "Not when it comes to sex, you're not. I'm the one who's supposed to be here for you, not the other way around."

"This is different then." Cami declared. "This time around, it looks like we are going to have to be there for each other." Cami turned to go, and then at the last second looked back over her shoulder. "Now, I know it's just supposed to be Buffy and no fooling around, but do you think we could get him to let us take a peek at what he's bringing to the table? You know, in case it turns out he's only a one-inch wonder." Then she sailed out, laughing as Ziporah cracked up.

Chapter Thirteen

Evan heard the laughter coming from the kitchen and turned to look just as they came scampering into view. They had both changed into lounging clothes before he got there and their carefree smiles and comfortably sexy attire reignited the fire that had been banked within him. Cami with her lush curves was dressed in a pair of grey work-out sweats that weren't quite yoga pants. They were way too sexy to be termed just sweats, with the way they rode low on her hips and draped so lovingly over her remarkable ass, though. She had a slouchy cut-up pullover on top of it that he assumed she thought was modest because it was baggy. But it was slipping off her bare shoulders and drooping down in the front, showing him glimpses of the soft looking sports bra under it and even softer looking breasts.

Ziporah was dressed in what he liked to call God's gift to mankind: black skintight leggings. They clung to every toned and lithe inch of her– from the perfectly round globes of her high, tight ass, over her sleekly muscled thighs and down those mile long legs to her dainty bare feet. Instead of a loose fitting sweater like Cami, she had on a beat up tee shirt that at one time must have sported a band's logo or album cover, but now all he could make out was faded colors and a few letters. It was so worn it was almost no barrier at all and as she dropped onto the couch cushion next to him, the gentle wobble of her small, high breasts told him she wore nothing underneath.

It must be my birthday, he thought with an inner smile as Cami set the tray down in front of him and took a seat on his other side.

"So," Cami stated matter-of-factly as she palmed the remote. "Rules for Buffy-thon. You can talk when we do, but you can't get offended if we hush you. We only do it so you don't miss out on the best lines."

"Hmm-hmm." Ziporah poured Frangelico liqueur and vodka into a shot glass and handed it to him with a wedge of sugared lemon. "Rule number two, every time a vamp bares their fangs, bites someone or gets dusted, we take a shot." She licked her thumb and grinned at him when she caught him watching her do it.

"Oh!" Cami added with a bounce, "and let's also do one every time Giles cleans his glasses." Ziporah seconded the notion so he guessed that was that.

"What is this?" he asked, sniffing the nutty smelling drink in his hand.

"It's a chocolate cake shot," Z said.

"Don't ask me how lemon and hazelnut make chocolate flavor but it works. Yummy," Cami piped in as Z handed her the next shot, then made one for herself.

"Now." Both girls, loaded with their drinks and fruit, faced him with serious expressions as Z concluded. "Do you understand these rules as they have been explained to you?"

Evan measured them both in silence. They were playful and cute. He hadn't expected that. It was refreshing. He had been in the BDSM lifestyle for almost twelve years. That's a long time. So long that he'd forgotten how to just play with a woman. Since he'd discovered his first club at age twenty-two, all of his sex had been intense structured scenes, with women who only looked him in the eye when given permission and the only time he spent with them was within that scene.

Refreshing didn't even begin to cover what he was feeling right now; faced with two beautiful and intelligent women who were in the mood to play was like a precious gift.

He downed the shot while staring at them both, then took his time sucking the lemon and using his teeth to tear the flesh from the rind. He put the peel in his glass and sucked a dollop of sugar off his thumb. "Mmm, delicious." He sat forward and fixed himself another while they continued to watch his every move. "Let's do this."

They were on their fourth episode—the ladies had graciously decided to start from the beginning so he wouldn't be lost in story lines and plot twists—and Evan was having a blast. The show was surprisingly witty and well written. But, it was the women who had him so enchanted.

They laughed and spoke over most of it, shouting out lines with enough gusto to impress a Rocky Horror Picture Show fanatic. They drank like a couple of frat boys, throwing back the shots without hesitation and lining up the next round.

As the night wore on, they shared tidbits about themselves. Cami was a movie buff and Z had an obsession with romance novels.

They peppered him with good-natured probing about his life and the work that brought him to New York. He got a kick out of the wide-eyed reaction to his new line of business; all-organic grass-fed cattle. His was the largest ranch in Texas providing steroid-free beef, and he was in New York overseeing the new distribution side of it. "Most of America is content with what they get in the big chain stores. The general population sees organic as just a fad or sales gimmick," he said with exasperation. "The food industry has been poisoning us for so long, people just accept it and think anyone who questions the need for all of the pesticides and chemicals is just a conspiracy nut."

"Not me," Ziporah said with only a little slur in her voice. "I hate processed, packaged and pre-made garbage food. Homemade is the only way to go." She tilted her head to the side and added as an afterthought with a little nod, "Although, I don't always pick organic. It's not the money, even though it's more expensive. I get that it is because organic farms aren't big massive productions and so their costs are higher. I'm cool with that. It's that there isn't what I need all of the time. If I'm making eggplant Parmesan and there is no organic eggplant ... well? What can I do?"

"And organic meat is the hardest to get. Well, not really here in the city any more. It has caught on here. But back home? Almost impossible," Cami chimed in, leaned into his side and rested her hand on his ribcage. Ah, alcohol, he thought, *thank you*. She nodded up at him as though encouraging him to agree with her, but his mind had shut off the minute her hands had landed on him. Looking down into her not-so-focused eyes, all he wanted was to kiss her. To keep from doing just that, he looked to the television. "Look, that one's dusted–time for another round."

Ziporah and Cami had driven him crazy for the last hour. About a half hour into the first episode, they had snuggled up to his sides, brushing their breasts against his arms or rubbing their thighs along his. It was making it harder and harder for him to remember that they were new to the scene and this was not a BDSM club, so they were not simply his for the taking. Tonight was supposed to be just what it was, an icebreaker to get them all used to each other. The problem was he didn't want to stop there; he wanted more.

The mood was seriously hot. The show wasn't what had Evan so turned on. No, it was the women who did that. He was watching a campy vampire show full of dead teenagers, for crying out loud and yet, he was rock hard.

Cami was now snuggled-up under his arm and her thinly covered delicious body was a soft sensual overload of delight against his side. Although Z had started out the night sitting on the far end of the sofa, she was currently sitting so close he could feel the heat flowing from her body to his. He adjusted his position a fraction and ... yes, now his thigh was stretched along hers, and she didn't edge away. In fact, she leaned in closer and not a force on the planet could have stopped the smile that spread across his face. At this point, any victory, no matter how small, was worth a celebration.

Never one to play it safe or quit while he was ahead, Evan slowly moved his arm from the back of the couch and cupped the back of Z's neck with a firm caress. He watched her profile as he did, determined to stop if she gave any signs of distress. She didn't though. No, instead of stiffening or pulling away, Z tilted her head and closed her eyes with a soft whimper that made Evan's cock twitch in his jeans. He moved his touch up into her hair and began to massage the base of her scalp and the sound she made tightened every muscle in his body.

Cami got his attention just then when he felt her weight shift against him. She curled onto her side and slid her knee up against his hip. She was watching him touch Z, with her forehead resting on his shoulder and he knew she liked what she saw, because he could feel the hot puffs of her breath getting faster.

With his chin, Evan nudged Cami's face up. He wanted to see her eyes, to know that she wasn't spooked or threatened. To let her see in his that he intended to have them both. What he saw in her expression ratcheted up his desire tenfold and had him dipping his head to taste her.

Just as those full, sweet lips touched his, he felt Z stiffen and start to pull away. Evan reacted like the Dom he was and fisted his hand in her hair to hold her in place. He felt her initial resistance and then the melting arousal that followed after when her body went pliant and her breathing increased as he kissed and lapped at Cami's mouth, drinking in this first delicious taste of her.

That was as far as he would push them tonight. He wouldn't take things further without the ground rules of safe words and limits in place. The women had other ideas, however.

All resistance gone, Z leaned closer. He felt the barest touch of her cheek against his, then Cami shocked the hell out of him when he opened his eyes and saw her fingers stroke Z's jaw. Slowly, with eyes open and ready to stop if either of them tensed, Evan pulled back just enough to brush his lips against Z's. Cami shuddered and leaned in for more. Z then reached up and trailed her fingers along Cami's neck.

Evan used his free hand to cup Cami under her chin and brought the women cheek to cheek in front of him, then licked first Z's lips, then Cami's and back again.

"Open," he demanded in a voice gone hoarse with pent up passion. "Dammit, open for me, now." It sounded more plea than order to his ears, but he couldn't care less, because they did open for him and he fell into their kiss with a sound of hunger like he'd never made before.

His hands actually trembled as he held them captive for his mouth, tasting the sticky lemon-tainted sugar that clung to the corner of Z's mouth and Cami's bottom lip. Each woman had a unique flavor and scent, and combined they blew his fucking mind. They followed his lead as his kiss turned ravenous, all of them panting as the heat in the room turned tropical.

Sliding his grip on Cami to the back of her head, he urged her kiss to his neck, while he dove into his first full tasting of Z's mouth with a groan. Cami didn't hesitate and latched onto the sensitive area just below his ear with enough gusto to do Joss Whedon proud.

Even as chills from Cami's bite raced down his spine, the feel and taste of Z's mouth flooded him in a heady rush. Her kiss was scorching hot, her small tongue tangling with his as he swallowed her sighs of delight.

He was going to fuck them right here on the couch. He could see it in vivid detail. He would sit Cami on the back of the sofa and he would feast on her sweet pussy as he pounded into Z, who he would spread out on the cushions below. It was so clear and so visceral an image that his whole body shuddered and every muscle bunched in preparation of making it happen.

"Fuck!" He wrenched his head to the side with a gasp. "Stop. Girls, stop." They were panting and as worked up as he was, both of them moving in that sensual hip roll that all women seemed to do naturally. He tucked them in tight on either side of his neck with a hard clasp on the backs of their skulls. Fighting his nature, as well as theirs, to slow them all down. The puffs of their breathing and the two different yet equally appealing figures pressed into him wreaked havoc with his determination to hold back.

"Goddammit," he groaned in frustration, pulling them in even tighter. "God, ladies. I want you both so fucking bad right now." He kissed one damp forehead and then the other, breathing in each woman's scent and taste. "Too many shots. Too drunk, ladies. Too fucking drunk to take this step. Son of a bitch." Their hands were running over him, Z stroking his thighs and scraping her nails along the way, while Cami was running hers up and down his torso, stopping to make small circles over the hardened tips of his nipples.

His had started roaming, too. Learning their different shapes and curves. Ziporah was sleek and toned, like a dancer or swimmer, with firm muscle over the long subtle lines of her form. Cami was softer, fuller. She had a ripe and generous figure that filled and overflowed his questing hand.

Over their backs, sides and hips was all he allowed himself, though. When he explored them in full for the first time, he was going to have a clear head so nothing could be in the way of allowing him to relish every single touch and discovery.

"I want to see you both tomorrow. Talk to each other in the meantime, alright?" He gave a tug to their hair and they nodded, he was touched and aroused when they slid their hands across his body until they met over his belly button and linked fingers, a show of their bond. That they did it while still in his embrace caused a flare of heat to surge through him, and he knew if he didn't get out right now, he never would. So, with a last brief, hard kiss for each of them, he disentangled himself from their lovely limbs and reached for his jacket.

As he shrugged it on, he took one last look at them. They looked tipsy and tousled. Cami's baggy shirt was drooping completely off one shoulder so the full lush curve of one of her impressive breasts was bared to him with only the thin sheer cotton sports bra covering it. He could clearly see a deep rosy nipple poking out, just begging for his mouth. Z's thin tee was even worse for his peace of mind. Both her nipples stood out in stark relief in that flimsy thing and her legs were doing a sensuously slow scissoring along each other, an indication of just how worked up she'd gotten.

With a muttered curse, Evan turned on his heel and marched out the door. As he stood on the curb and waived down a cab, he was tormented by the echo of two different perfumes and the vibrating hum in his bones of unfulfilled desire. It would be a miracle if he managed to sleep a wink.

Chapter Fourteen

Cami pressed a hand to her tummy in the vain hope of stilling the trembling there. Her nerves were coming from so many different directions. After working every day at the tavern for months, Z had talked her into taking tonight off. She had a manager for a reason and she had been overdoing it for sure. However, they'd only been open for a short time and taking a Saturday off just felt wrong to her.

She looked around for the millionth time and saw the same thing she had every other time she did that, the place was perfect and there was nothing for her to do. Her manager and staff had everything under control so she was torturing herself unnecessarily.

The other worries had everything to do with why she was taking the night off. Evan. Master Evan, rather. She had a date with a Dom. A Dom who wanted not just her, but her best friend, also.

And therein lay her other worry. Ziporah had been side by side with her as she'd looked into the possibility that she was a sexual submissive. She'd gone on line and brought her books, and it was Ziporah who suggested she talk to Riley, Terryn and Zoe so she could get first-hand answers from experienced submissives. In all these months of research and extensive discussions, Ziporah had never given any indication that she felt the same way about herself. However, as Cami really thought about it, maybe she had. Maybe it was more than just being a supportive friend that had Z doing just as much research as Cami herself had. Was Z submissive too, and just couldn't see it? Couldn't face it? It would make a lot of sense. Cami had read that women in powerful, demanding jobs, especially if those jobs included decision making over the people around them, tended to turn toward submission in the bedroom. They needed and craved a place where they could let go and hand over the control to someone else. And now, here she was, ready to take this step with her and try it out so Cami wasn't facing this alone.

Every argument that Cami had come up with to dissuade Z had been answered with a calm and reasonable response. Long after Evan had left, the two of them had taken his advice and talked. Both of them had been shocked at how turned on they were. It blew Cami's mind that she had become so aroused over what was little more than a couple of kisses. There was no denying that Evan was a force to be reckoned with, but as potent as he was, he wasn't the only reason they'd been ready to combust. It was the three of them together.

Cami had no interest whatsoever in touching Z and she knew that Z felt the same about her, because they had discussed that quite openly thanks to the shots and years of friendship. But there was something so unbelievably tantalizing about kissing him at the same time. And when he'd run his mouth over her neck then Z's and back again? Cami shuddered at the resurgence of chills the memory brought. Threesomes, apparently, were now her thing. And Z's as well.

Good Lord, she'd never been as turned on in her life as she'd been last night. And Z had said it was the same for her. "You don't have to be a sub," she'd said with enthusiasm, "to know that what just happened here was freaking hawt!"

Tonight, there would be no booze to loosen the nerves or hide behind. Tonight, unless something happened to derail the path they were on, the three of them would be having sex. "Oh God." With a hand on her somersaulting tummy, Cami headed for the door and an adventure of a lifetime.

Chapter Fifteen

Evan was nervous. As he admitted that to himself, he pursed his lips and nodded his head a little. Hmm, he was a seasoned Dom with twelve years of BDSM experience under his belt. However, as he stood gazing down at Manhattan from his penthouse, he acknowledged that taking on not just one, but two novices at the same time, was a first.

Because neither one of them was interested in exhibition at this stage in the game and they knew enough about him from Gage and the others to trust him, they had agreed to meet at his place. Evan was keeping the mood casual in faded blue jeans, a white button up shirt and bare feet. He hoped that would set the tone for the evening and put the women at ease right from the moment they stepped in the door.

Just when he was about to check his watch for the dozenth time, the bell rang. With one hand he pressed the buzzer to allow them up and the other he ran over the smooth skin of his scalp before he made his way to the door to let them in. "And, we're off."

The sight on his doorstep was like a kick to the solar plexus. Both were stunningly beautiful in their own unique way, and together they made a vision that just about brought him to his knees.

Ziporah was willowy in build and full sensual lips and big doe eyes highlighted her lovely face. Her dark hair framed her face perfectly, with the ends swooping in just under her delicately pointed chin. She was dressed to kill in a classic little black dress that left her arms and most of her amazing legs bare.

Cami was her polar opposite. She was fair skinned and her long blonde hair was a cluster of waves surrounding her beautiful face and cascading down her back. Her hourglass figure was the stuff of wet dreams, and she had that killer body displayed to perfection in a fitted navy blue skirt that fell just shy of her knees, with a high-riding slit up one side. She had a soft white sweater on that outlined and emphasized the abundance of her figure with a gleaming trail of pearl like buttons marching down the center, and Evan wondered how in the hell she made it through the streets of New York unmolested.

Whereas he had dressed to put them at ease, they had obviously dressed to impress. And it worked. He was more than impressed, he was blown away. He stepped back and motioned them ahead of him.

"Welcome to my home, ladies." He shut the door and then, before they could reach the living room, he maneuvered in front of them to give his first instruction. "You both look amazing tonight. About knocked me to my knees when I opened the door and saw you two standing there. I especially love your shoes, but as of this moment, I need them off. Hang your bags and jackets on the coat tree and leave your shoes on the floor beside it." They hesitated for a brief second and then turned to do his bidding as one.

"From now on, neither of you will wear shoes when you are with me as subs. It will be a clear sign that we are in a scene. You can also use that as a signal to let me know you'd like to begin a scene with me. Wherever we are, if you want my attention on an intimate level, ladies, all you need do is remove your shoes."

He watched as they absorbed that notion and exchanged glances. Once they were finished, he turned and left them to follow him into the sunken living room. As he took a seat on one of the overstuffed chairs, he motioned to the sofa in front of him. "Have a seat. There will be times I will require one or both of you to kneel or sit on the floor, but unless I specifically instruct you or you hear me say 'high protocol', you may feel free to sit any where you please." He indicated the tray he had sitting on the coffee table between them. "Would either of you like something to drink? A snack?"

"No, thank you, goodness I couldn't eat a thing right now," Cami said, fluttering her hands at her waist. Ziporah just shook her head silently. Evan leveled a look at her. "Ziporah, sugar," he said, "when you are in my presence as my sub, I expect all answers to be verbal. Understood?"

Her eyes shot up to him and he watched with amusement as they first widened in pleased shock, then when she caught herself enjoying his directive, they narrowed in rebellion. *Interesting*.

"Yes. Understood." She looked as though she was going to leave it at that snippy little remark then Cami jabbed her in the side. "No, thank you, I'm not hungry either." And she jabbed Cami back. Evan coughed to hide his laugh.

"Well then." Evan leaned forward and braced his elbows on his knees. "Let's talk safe words. Zoe and I didn't get into details when she spoke with me and I never got the chance to speak with Terryn either. Besides, it's best I hear those things straight from the both of you, rather than second hand.

"Have you two decided on a safe word?"

EMBRACING THE FALL

They looked at each other and shared a smirk, so he knew he was in for a treat before they even opened their mouths. He was not disappointed. "T-Rex," they said in unison. He was laughing full out by the time Cami got done explaining how she'd come up with that from being left alone on the dance floor with him.

"All right," he agreed as he tried to catch his breath, "I think that is even more ridiculous than Terryn and her pickles, but I like it. T-Rex it is. Now, then if you are gagged and can't speak, it's three sharp knocks on a hard surface, or if there is no hard surface I will place a red ball in your hands that you will hang onto and if you drop it, that will be your safe word signal. As far as hard and soft limits and what you'll both be comfortable doing, let me just say that I understand this is new for you and I will proceed accordingly. Feel free to use your safe word freely as we get started and I'll make adjustments as I go. Any questions so far?"

"No, Sir," Cami murmured sweetly, her eyes lowered and her hands in her lap.

"Nope," Ziporah snapped like a sullen teenager who'd just been grounded.

"Well, now." Evan sat back and considered her. Under normal circumstances he would have walked away and refused to scene with a sub so bent on insolence. But, a normal sub would never act that way, or would only do so in hopes of incurring a punishment. "Ziporah, answer me again." He reached to the chair adjacent to the one he was sitting on for a decorative pillow and tossed it on the floor by his feet. "But do it from here." He watched as, yet again, the first emotion that filled her chocolate brown eyes was surprised curiosity that was then chased away by stubborn determination. She slapped both hands onto the couch on either sides of her then pushed herself to her feet with a huff.

"Stop." *Don't go down without a fight, do you sugar?* "Crawl here on your hands and knees." He didn't take his eyes off of her and his look dared her not to defy him, but to obey him. There was a world of difference between the two.

"Yes, Sir." With ill grace, she slid to her knees then crouched to all fours. She put every muscle she owned to work so that she came at him like a stalking cat and the look in her eyes now was hot enough to scald. He said nothing until she was kneeling and she spoke her required, "No, Sir, no questions."

Then he cupped that stubborn pointed chin in his hand and asked her, "Do you consider yourself meek, Ziporah?" She all but snorted as she rolled her eyes and answered, "No, Sir. Not at all."

"I'm wondering something. Do you know why they use that term to describe horses?" Her brows furrowed as though she was wondering why the hell he was talking about horses at a time like this, but he waited for her to answer him. "Um, no. No, I don't." When he continued to wait she muttered an impatient, "Sir."

"Meek is often mistaken for weak. But to meek a horse means to train it without breaking it. Imagine a wild stallion, all that fire, all that passion. All that energy and life wrapped up in a thousand pounds of thundering muscle." He stroked his fingers along her jaw as he spoke, careful to keep the eye contact between them. "Now, imagine all of that majestic power coming under control. Not broken, not defeated, but with the gentle and firm hand of someone worthy, mastered."

Her reluctance melted and her lips parted on a small 'o' of surprise. That was key for her, he saw.

"I am not blind or a fool, sugar. You're neither weak nor spineless, I wouldn't be here if either of you were. I see your strength Ziporah; I see the core of steel within you and the fire. Last thing in the world I want to do is break you." He leaned down and brushed a soft kiss across her still parted lips then drank in the sigh she breathed like it was fine wine. "But, I will master you. Make no mistake about that."

Cami was about to combust right where she sat. Watching Z crawl to Evan, with her shoulders and hips rolling, while he'd sat there in his big chair and his gorgeous face all intense and focused had been such a turn on. Then, when he'd started speaking, it had taken all her will power to keep from moaning. This was what she'd been hoping for. In one speech, Evan had dispelled one of hers and Z's biggest fears. He didn't see them as footstools or weaklings. It was sexy as all get out.

Chapter Sixteen

"Cami." His gaze slowly lifted until he was looking her right in the eye.

"Yes, Sir?" she answered, though her throat had closed up with his attention zeroed in on her like that.

"Come with me, darlin'." Then he stood to his impressive height and reached a hand out to her. She stood immediately, not wanting to give him a reason to make her crawl wherever it was they were going, but she was frightened of leaving Ziporah. He smiled at her and his expression was softer than the one he used for Z. "C'mon, darlin'. I'm just gonna get you set up and then I'll come back for Ziporah once I've got you ready." Her hand may be shaking, but she still placed it in his, so that was progress. She was scared, but it was an exhilarated scared, like a roller coaster or a haunted house. She could handle this and she trusted him to stop if she used her safe word. So, as he led her down the hall, she followed him with only one wide-eyed glance back at her friend. Z looked concerned for her, so to ease that worry, Cami stuck her tongue out, then felt her cheeks burst into flames when she turned to look where she was going and saw that Evan had watched her acting like a fourth grader.

"Oops. Sorry, Sir," she said as mortification swamped her. Great, the man was leading her into a room for sex and he'd just caught her behaving like an infant. *Real sexy there Cam*, she thought to herself, real sexy.

"Sorry? What're you sorry for?" He backed her up against the door at the end of the hall and pressed all that big hard body into hers. "I like your playful side. You can stick your tasty little tongue out at her all you want, brat." He kissed her then and he was even more hot and delicious than she remembered. "Just remember, you stick it out at me and I'll be putting it to work." Then on that ominous note, he reached behind her and turned the knob.

"Oh, my goodness." It was a sex room. More than that, it was a BDSM sex room. There was a giant X on one side of the room that looked like it was covered in red padded leather. There was a spanking bench and a scary looking contraption that appeared to be an old fashioned stockade. There were bars and chains hanging from the ceiling in one section of the room and a giant, king-sized four-poster bed dominated the far side of the room, in front of the massive windows. A chest close to the door, big as a steamer trunk, caught her eye and she didn't want to even guess what was in there.

He stood behind her as she took it all in, quiet as she gazed around. He combed his fingers through her hair, tugging lightly and letting his nails scrape just a bit along her scalp. It was just a little disconcerting to be faced with the reality of it all. Yet he must have guessed that it would be, because even as her heart raced at each tool and implement she spotted, his touch soothed her.

"It's a lot to take in," he whispered in her ear, "isn't it?" Even as she answered in her own hushed voice that it was, he was gathering her hair to drape over one shoulder. His lips were soft, moist and hot and they set off a shower of chills when he laid them on that tender spot just behind her ear.

He stayed there for an eternity. His breath became the rhythm of her heartbeat, a slow hot pumping that calmed her nerves and awakened desire. What was it, she wondered, that was so incredibly exciting about a man breathing in her ear? Was it the unbelievable intimacy of being that close to another human being? Or was it the primal life force of each exhale that flowed from deep within him out and over that ultra sensitive shell? Whatever it was, it was killing her slowly as she waited for him to begin.

Just the slightest movement, a deeper pressure from his lips and a soft brush of his nose in the downy hair there and it brought a moan to her lips. "Cami, sweet brat." He spoke with barely a sound. "Unbutton your sweater." Her hands lifted without conscious thought on her part; they simply moved to obey his command. As each small pearl slipped free, she felt an answering kiss on her neck until there were no more and her hands were clutching at the cashmere, waiting for his next directive.

"Hands at your sides, now." They dropped to her sides so swiftly he chuckled. "Good girl." Then he was sliding the garment from her shoulders and off. He walked to face her, the top dangling from his hand and his gaze was ravenous as he stared at her in her high-waisted skirt and white lacy bra. "Hand me the skirt now." He looked fierce as he watched her hands fumble clumsily at the side fastening. Cami almost whimpered when the stubborn thing finally gave and she pulled the zipper down hastily. It was a tight fit so it took some shimmying to get it over her hips, but he didn't seem to mind. He watched as her breasts wobbled in their lace cups and it was obvious from his expression, he enjoyed the sight.

"You have a beautiful body, Cami," he told her once she'd handed him her skirt and stood before him in nothing but a white lace thong and bra.

"Thank you, Sir." She wanted to cross her arms over herself but knew that would only make her seem self-conscious, and the thought made her smile ruefully.

"What?" he asked.

"Sir?" She looked at him with brows raised in question.

"I know what brought the pretty flush to your face, but what brought the smile?" he questioned as he brushed the backs of his fingers over one heated cheek.

"Oh, that," she said in a bashful tone. "Well, I was feeling very exposed and embarrassed and wanted to cover myself with my arms. But then I was embarrassed about being embarrassed." She looked up at him with a face she was sure that was now as beet-red as a cooked lobster. "It's exhausting being me." There was that warm chuckle of his again, like honey-flavored crack for the ears.

"You're adorable, little brat." He kissed her then, his mouth swallowing up her gasp and feeding her back his soft groan as their tongues tangled and lips melded. Cami was just on the verge of stiffening up when he pulled away with a soft hungry sound and told her, "Go kneel on the right side of the bed and lay your upper body on it." Her hands went to her tummy, this time not to cover it but to try and control the frogs that had started leaping around in there. Once she was at the side of the bed she noticed a padded bench along the floor. It looked like one you'd see in a church for parishioners to cushion their knees while they prayed and Cami was touched by its presence. Comfort wasn't something that she expected Doms to consider a priority, so it gave her hope that he wasn't going to be quite as extreme as she had feared.

"Good girl. I want you to turn your face to the left so you can see the room. Good. Arms out to your sides on the bed. Come on. Full out. Stretch them as far as you can. That's the way. Now, palms up. Perfect." He stood behind her and ran one hand, firm and strong, along the center of her back, all the way down over the crease of her ass cheeks. Even as she felt a new flush of embarrassment, she also felt a rush of arousal at being seen and handled so familiarly. "Stay exactly where I've put you, Cami. I'm going to fetch Z and when we come in, you're to watch, but I don't want you to speak unless I give you permission." He waited until he heard her breathless, "Yes, Sir," before leaving, and Cami wondered if it was possible to die from arousal overload.

Cami half expected Z to enter the room on hands and knees but she walked in with her head high and her back straight. It was her kick-ass lawyer walk and the look on her faced matched it. It was the look she wore in front of juries and hardened criminals; and it dared any and all of them to cross her.

Z didn't stop to gaze around the room like Cami had; instead she sauntered right to the middle of it, then stood as straight and proud as a soldier waiting for Evan to decide what to do with her. Cami envied her bravado; Z had always had a beautiful knack of facing anything new or scary with a *Charlie's Angels* hair toss and a pirate's grin.

Evan started walking in slow circles around Z. His hands clasped behind his back and his eyes coursing over her from top to bottom the whole time in a never-ending journey while she stared straight ahead and tried to look unaffected. Cami noticed that he brushed up against her here and there as he did and she thought again of his reference to horses.

She'd seen a documentary once about a breeder of Friesian horses who refused to use artificial insemination to impregnate his beautiful stock. In one scene they had shown the mating.

The solid black stallion with his flowing mane and tail had stalked his eager and waiting mate in just the same way Evan was doing to Z. The male had circled the smaller mare, bumping her in challenge then nipping and breathing on her neck until she'd gentled and settled and then finally, lowered her proud and lovely head to let him claim what was his for the taking.

It had been primal and riveting. And right now, Cami couldn't help but compare the two scenes side by side especially as–holy crap! Evan leaned in and bit Z right on the neck. Not a kiss or a word first, just leaned right in from behind and laid his teeth to her.

Cami didn't know whose gasp was louder, hers or Z's. Ziporah's frozen and cool facade blasted away and the two of them locked eyes briefly as the other woman's hands fluttered up to clutch at her chest, then fell back at her sides when Evan growled a muffled, "Drop 'em," around his bite.

Cami felt her own neck tingling as she watched Evan crowd even closer, till he was flush against her back and then he lifted his head. Even from where she was, she could clearly see the glistening indentations left by his teeth in the delicate skin of Z's throat. He'd done it right over her pulse, and thanks to the mark that acted like a spotlight, she could see that pulse rabbiting. As fast as it was, Cami thought hers was probably faster. Freaking hell, that was hot.

Evan's tanned head gleamed in the lights as he towered over her friend and his emerald eyes were so vivid they looked like jewels in truth. Passion had marked his features as clearly as a chameleon changes colors. Gone was the confident and charismatic southern gentleman. Here and now, Cami was staring at the hard core Dom and it rocked her world on its axis.

"Cami, my sweet brat." It took a moment for Cami to realize he was talking to her, because he was staring at his bite mark on Z while he traced one finger over it in a long, slow circle.

"Um, y-yes, Sir?" Cami barely managed to get out.

"Will you please tell Z here how your clothes were removed?" Still without looking up and still tracing those marks. Cami felt her own neck arch in an unintentional invitation.

"You-you had me remove them, Sir." Cami swallowed and arched again. It was becoming hard to stay still.

"Do you know why I had you take them off?" He dipped his head and kissed the mark and Cami shuddered, or maybe it was Z, she couldn't tell any more. "Or why I am not going to allow Ziporah to do the same?" Z stiffened, then his big calloused hands gripped her arms tight and he tugged her to the tips of her toes as her eyes widened in alarm until they took up her whole face.

"Umm, n-n-no Sir." Cami had no idea sex caused stuttering but apparently for her it did. "I d-don't know why, Sir."

"For some women," he growled as he let Z's heels slam back onto the floor and fisted her hair in one hand to yank it out of his way. "The charge–" one hand tore at the zipper in the back, "comes from the strip tease." His eyes locked on Cami's and seared her soul. "Shedding the shy little girl and letting the sex goddess out to play." Her breath caught and she thought *yes! Oh God, yes!* "Now, for others–" He released Z's hair with a hard turn of his wrist that had Z gasping and used both hands to tug and yank her dress not just down, but off. "For others, the charge comes from pure–" Next he ripped her strapless bra off and flung it away, "brute–" Her panties were next, and for those he gripped the delicate lace of the thong by reaching his hands around her and grasping them right over the crotch, "strength." He tore them to shreds and Z was moaning audibly as he pulled the tatters from her then bundled them into a wad that he stuffed in her mouth. Cami didn't realize that her own mouth was hanging open in envy until it snapped shut when Evan looked at her.

"Fucking beautiful," he said when he turned Z to face him. Evan fisted one hand in her hair and the fingers of his other hand brushed over her lips and the lace that was stuffed between them. "So beautiful like this, sweet Ziporah." She whimpered for him at that and Cami saw the corners of his eyes crinkle in an almost smile. "I see you like being gagged as much as I like gagging you, huh sugar?" He did something then that almost made Cami come. He leaned forward and sniffed at the panties caught in Z's teeth and *Mmmm'd* in pleasure. With his nose nudging at her lips in teasing brushes, he continued. "But, unfortunately, I'm not gagging you tonight. Not on our first night of play." Then he snapped his own teeth on a bit of lace that was dangling out and slowly, inch by miniscule inch, dragged them from her mouth. The way he then tossed his head and let them fly could only be described as rakish, and it was just one more mind-blowing image to go with the thousands she had stored up already ... and they had barely gotten started.

Chapter Seventeen

Evan felt himself doing something he rarely did this early in a scene; he was hitting top space. It was that perfect head zone that took his entire being and narrowed every cell and atom in his body until they focused on his subs. He now breathed for them. His very heart beat for them. He was hyper aware of every nuance in their expressions and twitch of their muscles. Even his sense of smell was enhanced and he could pick up not only their individual perfumes, but the different scent of each of their arousals as well.

He marched Ziporah to the bedside opposite Cami and shoved her to her knees, because she needed his mastery over her body as surely as Cami had needed his mastery over her will.

They called to two different sides of him and though he had scened on several occasions with multiple subs, there was something different about these two. Something elemental that added a deeper level of importance and heat to the moment that he could neither explain nor deny. The difference between all the other women he'd had and the two he faced now? It was like comparing cannon fire to the pop of a cap gun.

With a hand on the back of her head and another between her shoulder blades, he flattened her out in the same position as Cami and locked eyes with her as he did. Cami was audibly panting and her pupils were the size of dinner plates. He bared his teeth at her in a smile that was just a little feral; her eyelids lowered and her body loosened in an unconscious offer of surrender. He could picture himself climbing across the bed on all fours and taking her right then; the sight of her submission so turned him on.

He had picked up on a lot from his little chat with Zoe the other morning and one thing had caught and held in his mind. Cami had been watching scenes, live and in person, for almost a year. His little small-town angel was a voyeur. That's why he had instructed her to watch them and why he would make sure she always did when it was the three of them together. Watching was one of her triggers and from the look of her right now, a pretty fucking big one at that.

He swallowed a curse as he pushed back his body's demands and strode to the chest by the door. He dug around until he found what was needed then went to stand at the foot of the bed and for a moment just stared at the erotic sight before him. Two beautiful examples of woman, one fair and full, the other dark and slight, bent over his bed on opposite sides in willing surrender, awaiting his pleasure.

He dropped the tools he had fetched on the bed between them and shed his shirt with impatient hands as they panted and watched, both sets of eyes tracking his every move.

The first things he picked up were the nipple clamps and though neither girl uttered a word, he distinctly heard them both swallow. Loudly.

"Up on your elbows, both of you." They moved in unison and Evan took a moment to enjoy the view. "Cami, sweet brat, remove your bra and throw it to the side." She sat back further on her knees to do his bidding and Evan felt his mouth water at the sight when those full, luscious breasts were finally freed. They were glorious. Unlike implants, her natural breasts had a lovely teardrop shape, with dark pink nipples sitting high and proud atop them. He studied them in silence as she flushed and fought to keep her hands to her sides. It pleased him tremendously the way she battled her own nature for him. For all of them. "Beautiful, way too beautiful for words, sweetheart. Now back down to your elbows."

He crouched down until he was squatting at the foot of the bed and leaned first toward Ziporah. He kissed her then, full and hard, delving his tongue deep into the depths of her mouth and tangling with hers. While he did, he ran the rubber tip of one of the clamps back and forth and around and around her right nipple. He ended the kiss at the same time he snapped the clamp on the small, pert crest. Her 'oh' of surprise was a warm breeze across his cheek.

Evan was not at all surprised to see Cami's eyes glued to them when he turned his head and swooped in to taste her mouth next. Her rich, throaty moan filled his gut and fed him like manna from heaven. Her breasts were so much larger than Z's that his hand was sandwiched between it and the mattress as he teased her left nipple the way he had with her friend's. But that rosy flesh was just as tightly puckered and when the clamp eased closed on it, he was again fed one of those sexy moans of hers.

He turned back to Z for the next and then again to Cami, and when he straightened he watched as it took a moment of bafflement for his subs to realize they'd been clamped ... to each other. Right to left and left to right. One couldn't move or shift without it affecting the other and as he watched them test it out, their reactions caused his already hard cock to throb.

"See, in my opinion," he said with a calm he didn't come close to feeling, "this here is the best type of restraint. You are not bound by ropes or cuffs you can fight, but rather by yourselves." He reached between them to where the chains crisscrossed and tugged a little, it was like a shot of whisky when they both moaned for him. "You wanna thrash and move. By all means go right ahead." He tugged a little harder and though both women moaned again, they also showed small signs of discomfort. Cami not so much with only a tightening at the corners of her eyes and Z a little more, she was biting her lip.

"Back down how you were. That's right, palms up Z, sugar. There you go."

He picked up the last item he had laid between them and a myriad of emotions flickered across their faces as he ran the leather strands of his flogger between his fingers. They were intrigued– Cami was getting a little scared, while Z was getting a little pissed. He figured he should get to it before their minds outran their bodies and stole their pleasure away with fears and doubt.

He started with slow, long strokes. More a brushing down each woman's back than a strike, getting them accustomed to the feel and texture of the tool. It was a buffalo oiled flogger of forty strands, heavy for more of a thud strike than a sting. Its strands were longer and denser and as they lay across each woman's back; it practically obscured them from view.

Evan made exaggerated figure eights with his arm, alternating between them equally. It was a slow build that warmed not just their backs but his muscles as well. Harder and harder by increments so minute that he was sure they barely noticed that he was now hitting them with a good amount of force.

Evan noticed though. The slap of the multi-tailed flogger was like the hard patter of rain as it landed on their now pink skin and they were crying out with hot breathy moans at each hit. And they *both* cried out at every strike, because neither of them could help but jerk at the lash and that jerking tugged on the other woman's breasts as much as their own, so the sensations were layered and coming at them from all directions.

Evan widened his strike zone and started laying into their asses next. The sight of Z's tight muscled ass absorbing the first smack caused him to grit his teeth in an effort to keep going and not stop to devour that rounded flesh. Then when he hit Cami's softer, larger one and he watched the beautiful way it jiggled, he moaned as loud as they did.

He struck fast then. Fast and hard enough to have them both crying out in gasps with each turn. Lost in it now, lost in the sounds and the smells and the glorious sight as they writhed for him.

Finally, he was done. They were panting and whimpering and their backs and asses were glowing a soft light red. He'd gone easy on them and only awakened the nerves just below the surface and not gone too deep. They would feel every touch and brush against them for the next hour or so in heightened awareness and then it would fade. Some day he would take it further, so that sensitivity would linger for days, but tonight it wasn't about endurance, it was all about awakenings.

"Carefully, so as not to hurt each other," he instructed in a voice so horse he barely recognized it, "climb onto the bed till you meet in the middle then I want you on your knees with both your asses facing me. Cami, remove your panties first."

He swore low and lewd watching them obey him and once they were in position, he tore out of his jeans like they'd caught fire. Then he stopped and cursed in frustration.

"Son of a goddamn fucking bitch!" The girls startled and looked first at each other and then back at him in alarm. "Sorry, ladies," he said, rubbing a hand on his scalp. "Sorry. In my haste to get my hands on you two, we skipped two very important topics of discussion." They were both still dazed and teetering on the edge of subspace, so he had to keep back to be fair and not overwhelm them. Right now they weren't so far gone they couldn't think, so he had to keep them that way until this was clear. "Health records and birth control." He cursed as he watched more clarity come into their eyes, but that couldn't be helped. "I know Zoe assured you of my health and I'm taking you both on faith that you are clean and protected because Zoe would have never approached me if you weren't, Cami. So unless one of you says T-Rex, we are doing this now and we are doing it raw."

Both of them kept silent. "Thank fucking Christ," he muttered and climbed on the bed. When the taste of Cami's pussy filled his mouth and her screams filled his ears, he thought his head was going to explode with the pleasure of it. She was melted honey and wet silk on his tongue. As he lapped and drank from her, his hand found the nirvana that was Z's sweet cunt, and dipping his fingers in her was like plunging them into heaven. Her muscles clamped down on his pumping digits with a strength that made him crazed to feel it on his cock.

He wrapped his arms around two sets of hips, pressing them close to each other and pulling until they followed his urging and lifted those glorious asses higher and their heads dropped side by side to the mattress. Evan kissed and sucked and licked and bit his way across Cami's ass to Z's and when the taste of Z's pussy hit his tongue with her own unique and delicious flavor, he groaned and drank deep. Deeper, sucking her clit hard against the roof of his mouth and demolishing it with his tongue. She exploded into an orgasm and her release flowed down his chin like champagne.

He worked his way back to Cami and clamped his lips around her clit next. He pulled on it with hard suction and tormented it with the lash of his tongue and just like Z, Cami was defenseless. She screamed as she released and came against his relentless mouth, while he feasted like a man possessed.

Evan forced himself to pull back. Reining his lust back was like trying to rein in a rabid beast, but he managed. Barely. "Remove the clamps," he snarled as he shoved from the bed and marched back to the chest. He strode back to the bed with a new tool in hand and it took less than a second to plug it in and get back in position.

The bed was specially made and he had commissioned it himself to be equipped with outlets in each of the four posts for just such occasions, and if he'd been a little less turned on, he might have taken a moment to appreciate the feature. But he was too far gone, too focused on the women in front of him, to register any thought beyond them and their pleasure.

"Heads and shoulders down on the bed, both of you." They dropped like stones. "Asses higher. God, that's a gorgeous sight. Lord almighty. Higher." He first positioned his shaft at the threshold of Z's slick opening and the bulbous head of the massager on Cami's clit, then he spoke again.

"I'm going to test you ladies on your endurance. One of you will have this on your clit while the other gets my cock. The one with the wand May. Not. Come. Until the one with my cock does." He rubbed both his cock and the wand over them tauntingly as he waited for them to acknowledge the rules he'd set forth. Once they did, with shaky breathless voices, he flicked the power on the wand to low and slowly slid into Ziporah.

All three of them moaned in ecstasy. God the feel of her! She was hot as fire and tight as a virgin. Her snug little pussy sucked him in like a greedy mouth, and as he sank to the root, he could feel his eyes cross in delirium.

Cami was already nearing the edge of another climax. Her mewling grew in volume and her hips were pumping against the wand with increasing pressure. He in turn increased his thrusts into Z, harder and at a different angle with each plunge until–there it was–her body jolted as he found the hidden gem of her G-spot. He grabbed his control in a chokehold and clamped a fist on her flank to hold her in place so he could ruthlessly pound into that sweet, sweet spot again and again.

"Oh my God!" Cami's voice was about two octaves higher than normal and Evan could clearly hear the panic in it. "Oh my God ohmyGodohmyGodohmyGod–" It was one long jumbled word that grew an octave with each repetition. Evan pumped faster, challenged and determined that he would get Z there with her. Almost there, he thought, as Z's pussy started to tighten even more. Harder, he told himself, fucking harder. Then, "*Fuuuuck, yes!* Yes." Z clamped down on his shaft in rhythmic pulses that fried the circuits in his brain and he pumped faster and deeper to help her ride out the full measure of her climax as she clutched at the sheets and screamed. Not a moment too soon either, because Cami came unhinged and bore down on the wand hard as her own orgasm barreled out of her seconds later.

Evan pulled out and switched. "*Christ!*" Cami's cunt was swollen and still pulsing from her climax, and as Evan plowed in to the hilt, he was shaking with the strain of holding back. Z cried out as the fat pink ball of the wand landed on her still thrumming flesh. He flicked the speed up to medium and she cried out again. Then he started stroking in and out of Cami the same way he had with Z. Testing and searching with each thrust for that perfect, sweet spot. "There it is, little brat," he said with a satisfied hmm. "There it fucking is. Right–" He thrust hard and she screamed for him. "There." Harder still and she quivered and called out again.

She was volcano hot and wet as an over ripe peach as he pounded into her and the drenched-slap of his hips hitting hers was the drumbeat to the music of her cries. Z shifted her hips, trying to pull away, but Evan followed and pressed in harder. She hollered, calling out as she fought her peak and Evan upped the tempo of his thrusts yet again. His grip on Cami's succulent ass was bruising but that couldn't be helped. Not right now, not when everything about her was begging for his Dominance. She screamed and pushed back into him and Evan felt his eyes roll back in his head as she flailed her own head and cried out while she came and came and *fucking came* all over him. Z saw it, and with a grateful cry, gave in and her entire body shook as she found her release as well.

He was going to go again. He was going to go back and forth between them until they'd each had at least two more climaxes apiece. That was until he looked up and saw Z reach out and clutch at Cami's hand as she still floundered in her orgasm. Their fingers grappled and tangled together and the three of them were linked in that moment and it snapped the last thread of his control.

With a roar like he'd never made before, he came and he came hard. His hips thundered and the force of it shot Cami back into the teeming waves of another climax. He pressed harder with the vibe into Z, and somehow managed to flip it onto high, and she too shot back into overload and the three of them shook and panted and came. Endlessly.

When Cami burst into tears as the echo of aftershocks were still resounding through them all, Z shuttled herself closer and started to gather her in for a hug. Evan beat her to it and, with no apparent effort, scooped her up like a damsel against his chest. Z was flat on her stomach and looking back at her best friend cradled like a princess in the naked arms of a sex god. He shushed her quietly and gently kissed her forehead as he hugged her closer and his eyes lifted until he was looking directly at Z.

That look sizzled and gave the clear message that he wasn't through with either of them yet, this was just a pit stop and when she smiled a little at that thought, he sent her a slow and sexy as hell wink. "C'mon, brat," he said with gruff affection that caused Z's toes to curl. "Let's get you two settled and more comfortable." He managed to crawl to the head of the bed on his knees with an arm full of full-grown woman without looking silly, in fact, Z thought, he looked freaking hot as hell doing it. He laid Cami down as gentle as he would a sleeping child and reached for the bedside table, where Z saw a folded comforter was waiting. He laid it over her with a kiss then turned to Z.

She expected him to order her to scootch up, or at the very least invite her to join them politely. After all, she wasn't fragile like Cami and was perfectly capable of climbing into bed all by herself. She did not expect—at all—for him to crawl to where she was and scoop her up the same way he had Cami.

As he held her close and kissed her softly, she marveled that she wasn't laughing or demanding that she could move on her own. It wasn't like her to even accept this level of pampering, let alone bask in it the way she was. But, she did and she was. It felt heavenly to be cradled like this. She didn't feel like he was treating her as a weakling. No, she felt like he was cherishing her. That was crazy, she told herself, impossible. Impossible or not, that was all she felt pouring out of him right now as he brought her forward and laid her gently next to Cami. No other word fit so perfectly as that. *Cherish.*

"You just let all that out, sweet brat. Let it go. We got you," he told Cami in a voice that had deepened from sex. He brushed her hair back from her face then leaned over and kissed Z on her temple before spooning himself behind Cami. He slid one long muscled arm under both Cami's and Z's pillows, then tugged and shifted until the three of them were pressed tight, with Z and him facing each other over the still sniffling Cami. His other hand smoothed Cami's locks away from his face and tucked them over the top of the pillow and then he reached over her and tangled his fingers with Z's, making them a unit, and Z felt tears sting her own eyes. This night and this man were so much more than she had bargained for. As she held tight to the hand in hers, she wondered how she'd ever find the strength to leave when the time came.

Chapter Eighteen

Evan sat back at his desk and had to mentally berate himself for letting his mind wander ... again. This was an important business decision and if he didn't pay attention and get his facts straight, he could potentially cost his company millions. He could either go in with this man's proposal and fail to deliver on it, or he could pass on it and never get the opportunity again.

"I'm sorry," he hedged, "I want to make sure I get this right. Can you repeat that last part?" It didn't help that Evan was against bringing in an outside company to begin with. So he tried to clear his bias and give the man a chance. He was good looking, with his all-American charm and healthy build. He had a good face and although he was a bit thick, he didn't appear sloppy or out of shape. Evan couldn't find fault in his appearance or demeanor, so he listened to market trend reports and projected revenue and he shook off the prejudices as his own distraction and focused on the facts instead of his gut.

Pac-West Distributions was a good solid company and had decades' worth of experience under their belt. They were campaigning and campaigning hard, for the distribution rights to his grass-fed organic beef. They had the fleet and the trusted reputation for getting the work done, but he and his shareholders were on the fence. It was leaning hard toward Pac-West and one other company, but there was also Evan's idea to just take on the added expense of expanding their own distribution line and doing it all in-house.

The bean counters in accounting almost spontaneously combusted when he brought that idea up, what with the rising cost of health care and the added expense of the pension plan that he refused to lower for their own employees. Not to mention the cost of nearly tripling their equipment assets and upkeep, and each and every one of his accountants had about had a heart attack.

So, he was left doing something that made him extremely uncomfortable–bring in an outsider, and trust him with his family's business. Sure this man's company was also his family's and they too had a reputation to uphold as well, but was this just a job to the man sitting across from him? Something that paid his bills and sent him to a beach twice a year? Or was it a part of his soul, the way it was for Evan?

His childhood was spent on the ranches that had been a part of his family for generations that went back to when Texas first became part of the Union, for God's sake and bean counters or not, he wasn't going to make this decision based on dollars and cents alone.

"Well," he stood and reached a hand out to let him know the meeting was at an end, "I am liking what you have to bring to the table so far. Let's meet for dinner next week, after I've had a chance to go over your proposal in more detail and we'll talk more then."

"Thank you, sir." His handshake was firm and strong, so at least that was a plus.

"I hope you'll call if you have any questions and I'll make sure you get buzzed right through. You and this partnership are our top priority over at Pac-West, and I want you to know, we get this sealed and it will stay that way."

It was a good line, Evan thought, a little too slick and rehearsed but he appreciated the sentiment. "I'm glad to hear that. It was nice meeting you. I'm sorry, what was the name again?"

"Mark. Mark Wahlberg."

———◆◆◆———

Evan faced the rest of the day determined not to be distracted. The two women he had spent the weekend with, however, had other plans. They had taken his mind captive and there didn't appear to be anything he could do about it. So he gave in and shot off a text to Ziporah.

> *why can't I get your sexy ass out of my mind and between my teeth where it belongs?*

Then, because he was nothing if not fair, he sent one off to Cami next.

> *the taste of you lingers on my tongue and I'm craving you like an addict…*

He was on the phone with one of the ad agencies vying for their new line of business when Cami's text came through.

> *If the taste of me is still lingering on your tongue… I'd say you forgot to brush your teeth. ew.*

Evan then had to explain away his loud and abrupt laughter to the poor guy on the other end of the line and agreed to give him a meeting in person.

> *see why i call you brat?*

Ziporah responded next while he was shuffling his schedule with his assistant.

> *Apparently you can because just reading this has me ready to beg the judge for a recess and come running.*

Another text from her followed, close on the heels of the first.

> *And how in the hell you accomplished that in one weekend I do not know.*

He read each of those messages twice before answering, savoring her words of devotion and giving them the attention such remarks deserved.

> *oh, ziporah. this is why I call you sugar. never mind how prickly your exterior, inside you are all sweetness and heat.*

Two minutes later, as he was just heading in for a meeting, he got another text from Cami and had to stop and lean against his office door to collect himself for a moment. She sent him a selfie. And wow.
She was in her tavern and she'd pulled her hair into childish pigtails then laid on the red lipstick, shiny and thick. Her black button down blouse had been unbuttoned and she'd tied it between her breasts. He could clearly make out her nipples, so he knew she'd removed her bra as well. The little imp was sticking her tongue out at him. She had captioned the picture with only a single sentence.

> *I'll show you brat.*

"And I'll show you how a Dom responds to his brat," he muttered, as he pocketed his phone and headed out the door. "Call my one o'clock and push them to tomorrow," was all he said and sailed onto the elevator.

Haven was closed until two, so by his calculations, he had approximately thirty-two minutes to discipline his brat as he exited his cab and took the steps to the door in impatient strides.

He was just reaching for the handle when a full-figured and striking caramel-skinned woman opened it and came bustling out. She raised her eyebrows at him and he couldn't tell if the assessing look on her face was favorable or not. Evan opened his mouth to introduce himself, but she cut him off.

"I know who you are. Don't bother. I saw you sniffing around my Cam the other night. She seemed to like it, so it ain't none of my business that you're here in the middle of the work day, when decent people are about their business trying to make a living and raise their families and you got to come in here and get all up in her place of work where people *eat,* mind you, and if I come back after my break and see you went poking in my kitchen and left a mess, then I'm going to be *pissed*! Just try it and see–" she kept going. Even as she was buttoning up her coat and pulling on her hat, she was still muttering about how scandalous it was that he was there when he shouldn't be as she marched away in a huff. Evan thought he just might be in love.

Then all thoughts faded but one as he shut and locked the door behind him and walked inside. Cami was singing. Gone were the pigtails and bright red cheeks. She had readjusted her clothing and there was only a thin clear gloss on her full lips as they wrapped around the words of an old Patsy Cline number and made them alive once again.

In the dim lighting she sat atop a stool in the center of the stage and sang of heartache and a broken spirit like one who would know. That was the hidden key to Patsy's music. No matter how beautiful the voice, if the person singing didn't have that deep well of sadness to draw from, the songs just fell flat. But from Cami, god, Evan felt the sting of tears prick his throat at the terrible haunting beauty of it.

He stayed in the shadows as she sang but she knew he was there. Her eyes tracked his slow progress as he rounded the gleaming oak and brass bar. Her voice grew huskier and the wrenching sadness she'd poured into the music lifted, replaced note by note with a sultry undertone that told him she knew why he was there.

Chapter Nineteen

Cami watched Evan emerge from the shadows like a dream. His head gleamed in the scant light and she could just make out his silhouette at first. Tall, muscled man draped in a designer business suit that fit him to mouth-watering perfection, topped by one of those ankle length overcoats that probably cost a year's rent. He was mesmerizing.

Evan was making his way slowly across the dining area now, weaving in and out of the tables and shedding layers as he went. The overcoat carelessly tossed on a table. Next the jacket dropped over a chair. His tie he only loosened and the same with the top two buttons of his gleaming white shirt. When he got to the foot of the stage, his hands went to his belt and he drew it off with a hiss of leather as it slid like butter from its loops.

Slowly. So slowly it was like torture, he wrapped the buckle end of that delicious strip of cowhide around one fist and left more than half of it hanging at his side. She missed a note when his free hand went to the button of his slacks and she saw the potent proof of his arousal straining there.

With shaky hands, Cami set her guitar to the side and stared at him as he lowered his zipper, one tiny tooth at a time. "I believe I told you what I would do were you to ever stick your tongue out at me." The zipper down, his hand reached in, and through the fabric, Cami watched as he gripped and stroked himself. "Brat."

"Yes." Cami had to swallow. Twice. "Yes, Sir." Her eyes were glued to the motion of his hand. She was waiting for him to bring his shaft out, bring it out so she could clearly see him fist that hard flesh. He didn't though. He just continued to stroke it, while she could only guess what it looked like and wonder if it was getting harder the way she was getting wetter. She swallowed again and licked her lips. "Does my sweet brat want her Dom's cock?" The question brought her startled eyes up to his. The emerald glowed in the low lighting, compelling her, challenging her.

Fear tried to assert itself, but she fought it back and nodded. "Yes, Sir." Evan didn't instruct her to, but she wanted to give him the high protocol of a structured scene. Cami had found safety in the scenes they'd had on the weekend together. A separation from any sexual encounter she'd ever had before and that separation, that distinction, freed her. "Please, Sir," she begged, then she toed-off her shoes and slid to her knees on the stage before him. "Please."

His eyes closed and she watched the effect her supplication had on him. Evan's lips parted and the skin tightened on his face until his high cheekbones stood out in stark relief. He tilted his head to the side a fraction, as he seemed to bask for a moment while he took her submission in. Then Evan reached out with both hands, leaving himself still safely tucked inside his fly-damn him- and wrapped the belt around her neck. He fixed it high up, to just under her chin and she felt him adjusting behind her until he was satisfied with the fit. Back to holding the belt rolled around one clenched fist, he stroked her hair away from her face with his other hand and said, "Take out my cock, brat."

Her hands trembled as she answered and reached for him. The stage wasn't that high off the main floor and he was a tall man on top of that, so with her kneeling before him, it put her face at the perfect level for the task at hand. The clenching between her legs was so strong when she finally wrapped her hands around him, that she thought she might've just come. It felt like she'd been waiting her whole life to be here. In this spot. On her knees, with her Master's cock in her hands and her will in his.

Without a word, he pulled on the tether that was the belt, so she lowered her head and took him in. He was hot and slick and hard on her tongue. No playful licks or teasing, the moment was too charged for it; she felt ravenous. Cami dropped her hands to her sides, flattened her tongue, opened her throat and slid down until that blunt head was bumping her tonsils and closing her airways. At the end of herself, and yet still she pushed, pushed as though to swallow him in truth. He growled and she felt his free hand fist in her hair as he cursed and pulled her back up. She made a hungry noise and sucked her way back down as his thigh muscles clenched. When she was so far down she couldn't get him any farther, she worked her tongue on the underside where that fat vein pulsed against her and she heard him curse again, fervently.

She loved giving oral. Cami had discovered this about herself years ago. At first, she had assumed the reason was because it was one thing that hadn't been a part of that night. One sexual act that hadn't been tainted. However, as she had come to understand who she was sexually, a true fully submissive woman, she found that wasn't the case. Along with a large percentage of subs, Cami's pleasure was derived from service. Her own experience was enhanced exponentially by the knowledge that she was pleasing the one she was with. For a sub like her, the giving of pleasure was every bit as vital as the receiving of it.

So Cami lost herself in the slide of that hot shaft on her tongue. The heat and slick hardness of it was her reward, her proof that she was pleasing him and her lips pulled her back down greedily every time the fist in her hair and the belt around her neck pulled her up.

"God, baby girl," she heard him say, "you are so fucking good at this. God. That's it, brat, suck it, yeah, like that. Just. Like. That." Each word was punctuated with a hard thrust of his cock and Cami felt her hips echoing his. Thrusting and grinding, and she wished she could feel him in both places at once. "Hands, sweet brat. Put your hands on me now." An order she was overjoyed to obey. Her fingers slid up the long strong columns of his thighs until she reached the tops and then cupped the tight sensitive sack between them.

They were drawn tight to the base of him, an indication of how close he was to release and Cami relished and dreaded the end. Relished the fact that she could affect him and bring him to the brink so quickly. Dreaded the fact that soon it would be over, when she never wanted this to end.

Lightly, but not too lightly, she squeezed and pulled on that tender flesh as she increased the suction of her mouth and she felt the effect on him immediately. With a groan so deep and guttural she felt it like a thrust in her pussy, he came.

His fist tightened in her hair and the one holding her leash hauled her in flush against his body and kept her there. Seconds later, he exploded across her tongue and spilled, hot and bright as fire, down her throat.

Aftershocks were still ringing through his legs when she felt him draw her back. She resisted. Cami wanted more; she wanted to bring him again. Even as he chuckled at her tenacity, he gave a sharp yank on the belt as well as her hair. "Listen, sweet brat." He bent forward and kissed the crown of her head. "Obey."

She sat back on her heels and batted her eyelashes at him with a pout. "Okay. But I don't wanna." Her reward was more of his rich, soft laughter and another kiss. This one on her mouth, where he lingered and cupped her face in two strong and safe palms. As his breath flowed over her cheek, it felt like a caress and Cami felt centered in a way she never had before. She felt a quiet, a stillness of spirit that was unlike anything she'd ever known. *With one exception.* This same feeling was with her last weekend when the three of them were together. But there was an added element to those times that was missing here. She couldn't put her finger on it, but knew that it was there all the same. A frown quirked her brow as she thought about it.

"What's caused this?" His question was as gentle as the thumb he used to brush the wrinkle on her forehead.

"I loved this. I loved it so much." She wanted to assure him. "But? I don't know. I miss Z. Since we started this together, it feels like she should be here." She looked up at him and felt a knot form in her belly that he might be displeased somehow. "Is that wrong? Are you m–" her words were stopped by the press of his lips against hers again.

"Cami, sweet," he said, straightening up and removing the belt gently. "Feelings are never wrong. They just are. And as it happens, it pleases me that you miss her."

Surprise had her jolting a little as he rubbed and soothed her neck where the belt had dug in. "It does?"

"Yes, of course. Cami, this is new to you both. Not just the BDSM, but also sharing the same man. Imagine how difficult it would be if the two of you were jealous of each other? This wouldn't work, no matter how much she would want to help you grow or how badly you needed that help. If either of you were to get possessive, it would have to end." He leaned down and kissed at a particularly tender spot on her neck. "Poor baby, got bit there didn't you?" Then he kissed it again before he stood and began adjusting his clothes. "So, yes. Since the two of you have become extremely important to me in an extremely short amount of time, I'm very pleased that you miss her." One more lingering kiss. "Thank you for this, sweet brat. Now behave or else I'll be back."

Cami warmed from the inside out at that and wanted to bounce to her feet and straight into his arms. She restrained herself though. Perhaps it was that Z wasn't here, or maybe it just wasn't the time for it, but she stayed on her knees instead and watched with a dreamy smile as he gathered his things and left.

Chapter Twenty

"And then he just left?" Cami nodded and Z had to stop chopping zucchini in case she got so flustered she lopped off a finger. "God, that's freaking hot. Did he look back and give you a sizzling stare, or was it old western style where he just sauntered off into the sunset?"

"The wild west version." Cami laughed as she assured her. "And yeah, Z, it was. It was off the charts hot."

Z finished chopping and barely managed to spare her fingers. "I wish he would saunter in and out of my work and have his way with me." A laugh bubbled out of her as she pictured it. Evan, with his gleaming bald head and muscled build, bending her over her desk, or better yet, the witness stand while judge and jury watched.

"You want me to put the bread in the oven for you?"

"You touch my bread and I'll stab you," Z threatened with a wave of her knife. "Last time, you let the oven slam shut and it fell. Stick to the salad and be thankful I even let you in my kitchen."

"Sheesh. It only happened that one time." Cami grouched good-naturedly as she tore up lettuce. "And now I know not to slam the oven door, so it's not like I would do it again." Z didn't even bother replying to that. Cami was a complete failure in the kitchen and everyone who knew her accepted that sorry fact, including Cami. She made up for the lack of cooking skills by never complaining about the clean up. When they ate at home, Z cooked and she cleaned and that suited them both just fine.

"I'm about done here anyway." Z added the last of the vegetables to the soup that she'd thrown together and gave the pot a quick stir. Simple Italian sausage and veggie soup with some homemade rolls and dinner would be delish and perfect for a cold fall day.

Her phone buzzed where it sat on the counter and Z picked it up without looking to see who called. She just mumbled a quick hello as she tucked it between shoulder and ear and carefully placed the rolls in the preheated oven. Then groaned at herself when it sank in that it buzzed, not rang. Bread in, she straightened and fumbled the phone into her hands, feeling like a sap for being so caught up in visions of Evan that she didn't even know a text from a call.

The fact that the text just happened to be from him made her bare toes curl and her stomach flutter.

i got you something

She grinned and replied

Is it as good as what you got for C? Cuz that sounded pretty yummy.

With one foot braced on the inside of her other knee in one of her favorite yoga stances, Z balanced in the middle of her kitchen and stared at her phone like a smitten teen.

well, its at your door. go open it and see

With a squeal, she bounded out of the kitchen and hollered to Cami on the way. "Evan sent us a present!"

"He did? What?" Cami yelled from the dining room where she was setting the table.

Z flung open the door with all the zeal of a kid at Christmas, or in her case Chanukah, and there he was. Every bit as striking and debonair as Cary Grant or James Bond in his expensive suit, and holding a bazillion red roses, and Z was surprised she didn't spontaneously combust right there in her entry way.

Their eyes locked. Her mood went from playful to primal in a nanosecond.

"You really gotta work on your grammar when you text." She tried to brazen it through. Z knew he could clearly see the effect he had on her, but her contrary nature egged her on anyway. "I mean, come on. You did graduate, right? Or is it that you're too big and important to be bothered with little things like punctuation and capitalization?" She had more. She was warming up to the rant now, but he stepped in and crowded her against the wall. Those beautiful flowers fell to the floor without a glance from either of them, because next he plastered his mouth to hers. *And feasted.*

Hungry noises were rumbling up from his chest as his hands molded to her ass and ground her against his already hard cock. She kissed him back like it had been years since she'd seen him instead of days. When he urged one of her legs up and hooked her knee in his elbow, she groaned because he took full advantage of her wide open position, rubbing and thrusting where she was drenched and aching.

Ziporah grappled for the fastenings on his slacks, needing his flesh against hers. "Hands," Evan ordered in a harsh bark, even as his kiss continued to demolish her. "Hands flat on the wall." She whimpered and squeezed where she was still cupping him, hoping to make him forget. He bit hard at her tongue and held it trapped for one blinding second and her eyes popped open to stare into the brilliant green fire of his. "Hands. Now." The sting of the bite was a sizzling layer to what was already an inferno inside her, and the show of dominance made her whole body draw tight with need.

She placed her hands on the wall. As ordered.

Z was wearing her favorite pair of yoga pants, with only a thong underneath, and those ultra thin layers were no barrier at all. Evan lifted her leg a little higher and shifted his hips away from hers. She cried out at the loss, ready to beg but after that he put his hand there. Those thick, blunt fingers knew exactly where to go and he wasted no time with teasing or playfulness.

He pressed deep, then rubbed hard and fast right on the throbbing button of her clit. The friction, the surprise of seeing him after days of dreaming and then hearing the details of what happened at the tavern, all combined to catapult her into readiness. There was no holding back. There was no defense. Z was his in that moment, her body helpless to do anything but follow where he led and give what he demanded. When she came, she came screaming her orgasm into his mouth.

Evan held her through the aftershocks and tremors. Riding them out with her, so what would have been a quick, fiery blast bloomed into something much more profound and tender. Slowly, he let her leg down and it wasn't until her breathing was almost back to normal did he stop touching her and step away.

When he bent to scoop up the flowers, the smile he sent back to her over his shoulder was electric. "You can take your hands off the wall now, sugar." Ziporah burst out laughing. She had still been so dazed by what happened that she hadn't even noticed that they were still where he had ordered them to be. In an effort to try and get her equilibrium back, she put her hands on her hips and demanded, "What's with that 'hands on the wall' any way? I don't remember us giving you the green light to Dom us any time you please. Did I ask to be Dom'd, oh high and mighty, Sir?"

He didn't seem impressed by her show of pique, in fact, if anything, it made his smile bigger. "'Course you did, sugar." He passed the flowers off to her and kissed her softly on the temple. "You answered the door in your bare feet."

As he walked away chuckling, Ziporah looked down just to make sure, because if she were honest with herself, she had to admit she couldn't feel her feet at the moment. With her arms full to bursting with roses, she turned to shut the door, shocked to realize she was just now thinking of it–but, she saw it already was. He must've kicked it closed as he was getting started, but she'd been so overwhelmed she hadn't even noticed.

With a rueful shake of her head at her own besotted state, she headed back to the kitchen sniffing her flowers and knowing that she was never going to look at roses quite the same way again. When she turned into the dining room, Evan was just rounding the table toward Cami. Since his overcoat and jacket were gone, she assumed he'd detoured to leave them in the living room.

"Okay, I didn't peek," Cami said with color high and bright in her cheeks as Evan wrapped his big strong arms around her. "But that sounded seriously hot, you guys. Like wow."

"Look, Cam," Z gushed, "he brought us flowers. Should we feed him? We could just kick him back out into the cold, after all he wasn't even invited." Cami ooh'd over the flowers and then stopped with her hands on her hips to glare between the two of them.

"Wait a minute," she said with a pout on her face that made Z smirk. "Did you hear her? She is always smarting off to you. How come she's not the one you call brat?"

Z was curious as to this answer too and looked to Evan with one brow arched as she waited for what he would say.

"Because her smart ass remarks are all for show and she only pulls them out when I've got her rattled." He winked at Z when her mouth fell open, but she could think of nothing to say that wouldn't prove his point, so she snapped it right back shut.

"Now you, on the other hand, are only sweet and polite when you are thinkin' too hard about what is the proper thing to do or say. When your guard is down, sweet brat, you are a hellion."

Ziporah laughed so hard that she snorted and that got them all laughing. Evan was so perceptive, it was scary. That was so exactly spot on for both of them that she wondered briefly if he had a psych degree.

Cami looked as if she might be considering a comeback, now that the laughter had faded but then Z remembered, "My rolls!" She thrust her flowers at Cami and dashed to the kitchen.

"So," Z heard Cami say, "wanna stay for dinner." Then after a beat, "And sex?"

Z smiled as warmth filled her from the toes up. "It would be my pleasure, brat," he said.

Chapter Twenty-One

One week later, they were back at Evan's place. Due to work and circumstances, he hadn't been able to get his hands on these ladies for seven days, and the wait had driven him mad. Thoughts of them both had carried him throughout his days, leaving him in a constant state of semi-arousal. And visions of them, their bodies, their smiles, their laughter and their sighs and moans had filled his dreams.

They were in his sex cave, as Cami had taken to calling it, and Evan was basking in the sight before him. He had both women flat on their backs, side-by-side on his bed and restrained.

"Are you comfortable, sugar?" Evan asked, as he leaned over and brushed a lock of hair away from where it was caught in the corner of Z's lush, open red lips. Her big brown eyes were a little wild and uncertain as she nodded at him and mumbled a breathy, "Yes, Sir."

"Good." He kissed her on those juicy lips and moved his attention to Cami. Unlike Ziporah's, Cami's eyes were at half-mast and slumberous. Evan had been brought low by her reaction to being restrained. Each pass of his rope around her thighs, arms and waist had sent her deeper and deeper into subspace. She already looked well and truly fucked and all he'd done so far was tied them up.

He knew the answer, but he asked her anyway. "And how are you, sweet brat? You doin' okay?" Her answer was more moan and sigh than actual words and it brought a satisfied warmth to his heart, so he cupped her cheek briefly before standing back to survey his work.

Evan had decided to bind them together for this session. He had started by having them sit down close side-by-side on the edge of the bed and hold hands. First thing he did was wrap his rope around their waists and shoulders, cinching them tightly together, careful to make sure their breasts were left free for him to play with.

Once they were secure, with arms immobilized, he laid them back and started on their legs. Evan brought their knees up high against their bodies. He then weaved the rope in and out of their waist bindings until all their precious parts were open and exposed. Free and clear for him to play with.

"Ladies." Evan injected plenty of force behind his voice to make sure they heard him and registered what he was saying, especially Cami, considering she was already happily skipping toward subspace. "What is your safe word?"

"T-Rex," Z answered with a tremor in her voice that was equal parts fear and excitement. The Dom in him relished the sound. Cami only nodded with a mmm sound, so Evan sharpened his voice a bit more. "Cami, what is your safe word?" When her next response was the same, Evan used the riding crop in his hand to deliver a sharp smack right on the apple of her ass that the position had tilted nicely up for him. The sting of it jolted her entire body and snapped those sleepy, beautiful eyes wide open. "T-Rex, Sir."

"That's more like it, brat." Evan chuckled as she nodded and licked her lips. If he knew anything, he knew his little sweet brat was right now thinking up ways to get herself smacked again from the look on her face.

"There's something you two should know about me," Evan said as he started preparing his tools. "I love to play with my subs," he told them, plugging in first one Hitachi wand and then the other. "I love your bodies." Bending over, he picked up the container of clothespins he had hidden on the floor by the bed and laid it on Cami's stomach right above her belly button. "I love the way you smell." He leaned over and ran his nose up the inside of Z's thigh with a long, exaggerated sniff. "I love the way you taste." Just a shift of his head and he sunk his teeth into the flank of Cami's right hip. Her delirious moan was like music to him. "I love the way you feel." His hands reached forward and he squeezed one small tight perfect breast and one equally perfect large one. "But most of all ladies, I love the way you respond to me." He looked first into Cami's eyes and then Z's. "I love the way you come. So that's what tonight is going to be about. I want my subs to come for me. I want you to come and come and come and then come again. I want you to come until you're both drunk with it. I want to hear you screaming till your voices crack, and coming on my bed until it's drenched in your juices. I'm going to go all night, ladies, and your safe word is the only thing that's stopping me." He picked up a wand in each hand, stood so he was centered between their bodies and flicked the switches on with his thumbs. As the hum of the vibrators filled the air he said, "Now let's begin."

He placed the large fat balls of the vibrators right on their pussies and held them there without mercy, even though the women called out in surprise. As the feeling intensified, they began to try to squirm and move, but he had them hogtied good and proper and there was nowhere to go. It didn't surprise Evan at all that Cami was the first to break. She called out in soft breathy cries as the first climax poured out of her like a gift. He didn't remove the ball from her but he did move it down a little so it wasn't direct stimulation in order to give her space to recover.

Ziporah wasn't far behind Cami and in moments, her own cries were filling the air. She came with tiny jerks of her torso that made her small breasts wobble enticingly and Evan leaned between her legs to suckle them in appreciation.

Now that they had both been warmed up, so to speak, Evan turned and reached for the stands he had waiting behind him. They were custom-made stands just for this purpose. Similar to a microphone stand they held toys like these wands and were adjustable in so many delightful and practical ways. Evan first attached Cami's wand and adjusted the stand until it was directly where he needed it to be. Judging from the look on Ziporah's face, she had had enough time to recover now, so he next adjusted her wand and stand.

With a smile that felt just a little bit mean, he reached for the toys and upped the speed a notch. Their gasps were a harmony of delight. While his girls were panting and letting out whimpers of pleasure, Evan reached for the clothespins.

"You both have such lovely breasts. Perfect specimens for each taste." He leaned over Ziporah first and nuzzled along her left breast, kissing the soft underside around the sensitive area where breast and underarm met, noticing that she was a little bit ticklish.

"Z here, so perky and firm. A man can fit this whole lovely plum right in his mouth all at once." And that's just what Evan did. He opened wide and sucked her in, tonguing the hard-tipped morsel of her nipple. His mouth was too full to smile as she cried out and trembled for him, but the smile was there anyway. He lifted up his head just enough to give it a couple firm tugs with his teeth and flicks of his tongue.

When he opened his eyes, it was to see Cami watching him with a look of rapture on her face. God, it turned him on so much that she was a voyeur. That she loved watching was like adding a decadent dessert to a meal that was already a feast. He straightened and looked Ziporah in the eye. "Brace yourself, sugar." Evan brushed the clothespin teasingly back and forth across the wet, waiting nipple, then slid it over and gently clasped the edge of the breast where the armpit flowed gracefully into breast.

He walked over to Cami next and with one hand he cupped and massaged her left breast, while he reached his other hand back into the bucket. "And these beauties," Evan said with a pleased rumble in his voice, "are the other side of perfection; for when a man wants to gorge himself." And Evan did just that. He feasted, licking and sucking and biting his way over every inch of that generous and glorious flesh. When he pulled his mouth away, the entire mound was bright pink from his attention and the nipple was a hard rosy red. Just like on Z, he put the first clip where the breast formed at the edge of her chest. Then dipping back into the bucket, he fished out another pin and added it right next to the first.

Back and forth he went, lavishing kisses and suckling bites on both of them until the clothespins lined across their chests like a picket fence on a sandy beach. Meanwhile, those wands had continued to hum and buzz against pussies that had become completely soaked.

"Damn," Evan exclaimed when he stepped back to look at his handy work. "If this isn't the sexiest fucking thing I have ever seen. Fuck. You ladies floor me." He leaned over and kissed first Z and then Cami, full, wet, tongue-thrusting kisses that made all three of them groan and hunger for more.

Evan stood back up and reached for two more clothespins. "You get to go first this time, sweet brat." Moving the wand temporarily out of his way, Evan gently grasped one of her swollen pussy lips and used the clothespin on it to hold it back and out of the way. He did the same to the other side and now her clit was vulnerable and exposed. The pins had only moderate tension in their springs, but Evan still took the time to make sure they weren't pinching.

"Okay, sugar, your turn, brace yourself." Evan repeated the same steps on Z's tender labia that he had on Cami and then moved back. Taking up the wands in each of his hands, Evan spread his stance and braced his weight forward as though getting ready to charge into battle.

Slowly, with his eyes glued to the women bound and helpless before him, Evan lowered the bright colored rubber balls onto the flesh he had uncovered. Their screams were electric and poured into his body like a life-giving force. Neither of them could move, trapped in their bindings and helpless to do anything but take what he gave them, and he reveled in it.

"Oh God, oh God, oh God! Please, please, please, oh *please*! Oh God–" Z was screaming as her head thrashed back and forth and her feet pin wheeled, the only parts of her body that had freedom of movement, as the climax barreled down on her. Evan pushed just a fraction harder on her wand and rumbled out, "My name." He snarled in savage passion, "is not God, sub. Say *my* name." Then he turned up the speed on her wand and Ziporah lost her fucking mind. She came with a wail that reverberated off the walls and into his very soul. It went on and on. Christ, but she was beautiful in her passion.

"Oh *fuck*!" Cami's shout was so guttural the two words had at least a dozen syllables as her climax blasted into her. She groaned and arched her head back as far as her neck would allow and Evan could see every muscle in her body straining as it was caught in the throes of ecstasy. "Oh my God! Oh my God, *please*! It won't, it won't, it won–" Cami's body gave a mighty heave that jerked both her and Z. "Stop! Oh God, Sir, it won't stop." Her honey-blonde hair was a whirlwind around her face as she tried to thrash. "Coming. I'm still com-m-m-ming."

The groans and shouts she was making were driving Evan mad. There was a hunger inside him that could only be fed by this. *By them*. These two stunning women who laid themselves out bare for him. Who offered him everything. "Don't stop," he warned her in a voice he barely recognized. "Don't you dare fucking stop." Then he upped the speed even more.

Evan crouched down so he was eye level with what he was doing. He pressed for more from Cami even as he pulled back a little for Z. After an eternity, Cami's pleas dissolved into a scream of mindlessness and her body poured forth of rush of fluid as a brilliant orgasm washed through her and soaked the bed.

Staying right where he was, Evan focused again on Z as her body and moans showed signs that she was nearing peak again. "That's it baby," Evan crooned to her, "That's it. Gimme more. Fucking give me everything." She screamed and he heard her say, "I am," and he was lost. Lost in them both.

He stood up to his full height again and reached for the stands. As he adjusted them, this time from the outsides instead of from between their legs, he positioned the balls securely right over their clits, while he made sure to leave their holes free from obstruction and open for his play.

Z was already screaming in the throes of her next orgasm when he thrust his fingers inside her. She was molten hot and tight as the grip of a constrictor on his plunging digits. Cami's sweet cunt was just as hot and wet and tight, and Evan cursed viciously at the feel of the contractions still pulsing through her sheath.

"Fuck, ladies." Evan's voice was almost reverent. "So good, you both feel so fucking good. Again now. Go again, both of you. Right. Fucking. Now!" And they did. They came for him like fountains, raining in a scorching rush across his palms. "More," he demanded, endlessly greedy. "More and more and fucking more."

Chapter Twenty-Two

All three of them were sweating, the girls' makeup a ruined mess that he found sexy as hell. His arms pumped until his hands threatened to cramp and his biceps strained to the point of burning. He adjusted and readjusted the wands, never leaving them in the same place for long, so their bodies could in no way become immune to the stimulation they provided. He'd lost count of the number of orgasms he'd coaxed, won, and yanked from their bodies. It wasn't enough, he feared it would never be enough. They were his food, and he was ravenous.

To the chorus of women lost in subspace, Evan stood and reached for his riding crop. Their voices were an incessant symphony, an ongoing aria that filled the room with its erotic melody. With deft and precise flicks of his wrist, Evan aimed for the pretty, crooked row of pins across their breasts. Each flick of the crop popped off another one, and every time it did, the woman freed from that bite cried out for him. *Snap. Snap. Snap.* They sprang free in order, like dominoes falling in a line, and Evan wished he had taken the time to have added more.

"Oh ladies," Evan crooned as he removed the stands and the remaining clothespins from their labia. Then he took the wands in hand again. "What have you done to my control? I wanted to be here all night. Hearing you scream. Making you scream." Evan turned the speed on both toys up to full blast and laid those balls directly on top of each woman's left nipple. Right on cue they screamed for him. And it was magnificent. "But I need you now. I'm already there, already bursting to be inside you. And it's got to be right fucking now."

Evan placed himself between Cami's thighs, bent forward so he was a looming over her as she was restrained beneath him. With the shift of his hips, he nudged his cock forward, positioning himself for that deep slide within. "Look at me, sweet brat. My sweet, sweet brat." When those big blue eyes fluttered open, they were dazed.

"Oh, Sir. Oh my, Sir." Her head lifted as far as she could reach, her whole body begging for his kiss. Evan was helpless to deny her; he brought his mouth down and kissed her deep and wet and thoroughly as his body sank into hers.

It was like plunging his cock into wet wildfire, and that fire spread throughout his entire body. Without breaking their kiss, Evan placed one wand on one of her tender nipples and swallowed the cries she uttered like it was candy. With the other arm going by feel alone, he ran that undulating ball from one pert breast to the other as Z continued with her own cries.

With no warning to her, Evan changed the tilt of his thrust and started pounding that spot inside Cami that he knew would give him what he was after. One. Two. Three sharp fast strokes and her pussy clamped around him like a trap as her release flooded them both.

Her sheath was still pumping in aftershocks when he pulled away from her with a groan and thrust into Ziporah. "Heaven, sugar." Evan panted as he leaned down to taste her lips. "So fucking good, it's like heaven." And it was, her walls were tight, clinching and they ripped his control to shreds. He thrust faster, harder. Evan felt his lips curl back from his teeth in a wild show of passion when he straightened and let his hips fly.

Evan placed Ziporah's wand back on her clit and shouted at the instant clenching it caused around his cock. With Cami's, he placed it on her clit with his palm and pressed it tight while he thrust three fingers inside her. With hand and cock, he fucked them both like his life would end if he didn't.

Ziporah's body started to tighten up, racing toward another climax and that clenching around his shaft yanked the final thread of his control and obliterated any chance he had of holding back his own release. His hips powered into her faster, deeper, harder than he had before and as Ziporah released and flooded all over him, he did the same to her. Animal sounds of primal lust rumbled from his throat, as the blinding force of his climax exploded within him like a supernova.

By some miracle, Evan had managed to keep his hand and wand placed on Cami. Being who she was, experiencing the sights and sounds of the two of them coming, combined with the physical stimulation she was receiving, triggered a release for her as well. Cami bore down hard on his hand and screamed, as her own climax caught her up in a wave of heat and rapture.

As the strongest orgasm of his life began to fade away, Evan found himself struggling to stay on his feet. He felt drunk, drugged and detached from reality. His coordination was for shit when he tried to turn off the wands one-handed. Clumsily, he fumbled with them until he'd succeeded, then dropped them both to the floor to be cleaned up later. He fell forward and braced himself above the two women with a hand on either side of their heads and kissed them endlessly, passionately and reverently, as he mumbled words of praise and gratitude for this incomparable experience.

It took more effort than he would ever admit to sit them up and remove the ropes. The two of them leaned on each other like refugees and watched him with quiet, adoring eyes. It was the expression on those faces that propelled him and kept him going. Evan couldn't remember ever having this strong of a reaction to a scene before. Or feeling this deeply connected to a sub, let alone two. They were different. They were everything to him. He wanted to be worthy of the looks he was receiving. He wanted to be everything to them. He wanted to be fucking Superman for them. It was all he could do not to stumble on his way to get supplies to clean them up, but he did it; Superman didn't stumble. When he came back into the room, they were sitting where he'd left them and warm affection filled his heart at the sight.

"Poor little subbies." He chuckled at them. "Look at my girls. My beautiful girls. I'm the luckiest fucking bastard on the planet." Pleasure brought a becoming flush to faces that had started to cool as Evan placed the bowl of warm scented water on the bedside table and dipped the washcloth in it.

He continued to murmur to them, little words of praise and endearments, as he bathed their faces and washed away the smeared makeup and drying sweat from their skin. It took four washcloths and two separate bowls of water to get them cleaned up because he was thorough with his ladies. Aftercare was every bit as important as what went on before it. He washed under their arms and breasts, and was exceedingly delicate with the over stimulated flesh between their legs.

Once they were bathed to his satisfaction, Evan reached for the lotion next. The sweet scent of mangos and coconuts filled his nostrils and mixed with the lingering scent of sex, as he rubbed and massaged every inch of their torsos as well as their legs and arms where the ropes had bound them. "Won't do to have my girls showing rope burns. I take care of my angels, my sugar and my sweet brat. I take care of what's mine."

That night he'd carried them, one at a time, from the sex cave to his bedroom and tucked them into his own bed. And as he slept snuggled between two of the most beautiful and amazing women he'd ever been blessed to know, he didn't dwell on the fact that this was a first for him. Even back in Texas, Evan had never brought one of his subs or slaves into his personal space. He always figured that's what he had a bed in his playroom for; his personal space was his own. However, tonight there had been no question in his mind of where they would sleep. These two belonged in his bed and he was so content to have them there, it never even occurred to him to question it.

Chapter Twenty-Three

Meetings with stockholders and a lot of other things that didn't make a lot of sense to Ziporah, had kept Evan away for days. He called and texted both of them regularly and it was a fun and flirty way to get to know each other. Both she and Cami had talked about the fact that this was more than either of them had bargained for. They both realized this wasn't about sex or exploration. They were in a relationship, albeit not a traditional one by any stretch of the imagination, but they undeniably were. Surprisingly, neither one of them would have it any other way. They were both crazy about Evan and thrilled to every new experience he shared with them. But it was more than that; it was late nights watching Buffy and laughing at his good natured groaning. It was music, and long talks and heated debates on everything from politics to movies. Who knew if this could really work for anything long-term, but right now it worked like magic.

Z pressed the button for the elevator in the precinct and tried to keep the silly smile off of her face. Smitten or not, she was still an assistant district attorney for the city of New York and she had to look the part. Nothing could have pleased her more than seeing that beautiful, dashing bald man standing there when the doors slid open.

"Well isn't this a nice surprise." His rich southern drawl turned his words into music that hummed through her heart. "I thought you were in court today."

"Opposition was granted a reprieve." She narrowed her eyes as she said it, still fuming, because she knew it was just a delaying tactic by that shark defense lawyer. Evan chuckled at the look on her face and reached one hand out to help her in the elevator while the other prevented the doors from closing.

"I'll just consider this my lucky day then." Evan removed his hand and the doors slid shut, while he crowded her into the corner with a devilish grin on his face. She would never admit to him the way his smiles made her toes curl and her tummy flutter. No, she would never give him that. The man had too much mastery over her as it was.

"Why didn't you get off?" Her cheeks burned in a blush when he laughed huskily at that.

"Oh, I think I'll be getting to that right quick." She dodged his kiss with a laugh by ducking her head at the last second. She tried to shove away but she should've known that would be useless, he was much too strong for that.

"You know what I meant." More laughter as he tried for another kiss and she ducked the other way. "You didn't know I was going to be here, so why didn't you get off the elevator." She was going to get whiplash if they kept this up much longer.

"I was going to have lunch with your cousin, but I found something that looks a lot tastier right here. Now dammit, hold still and give me a bite." His hands cupped her face and his mouth descended. The kiss had just started, her lips barely parted, when the elevator dinged to signal a stop.

She sprung away with a jolt and tugged at her jacket, even as she tried to remember how to look professional. Three men piled into the car as she and Evan stood side-by-side in the back of it. The new occupants paid no attention to the two of them, deep in their own discussion about things Z didn't care to hear about.

She marveled that they were oblivious to the sexual tension thrumming through the air. There was a stillness, a predatory quietness to Evan that filled her with expectation. It was exhilarating. All those months when she had been researching with Cami and fascinated by what she was learning, she'd chalked it up to simple curiosity. Now, after all that she'd learned about herself since Evan had come into their lives, Z realized that it wasn't just Cami who was a sub, but herself as well. Exhilarating hardly described the giddy, hard to contain, joy she was feeling. Out of the corner of her eye, Z saw a muscle flex along his cheek and jaw line, indicating the extent of his arousal.

He looked as though the smallest nudge would snap his control. Ziporah's bubbe had a saying she was fond of that fit this moment perfectly. Never tug a tiger by its tail. As a child she had always wondered what would happen if she did. Still looking straight ahead, Z decided to try it and see, so she slipped out of her pumps.

Evan tensed so dramatically, Z was shocked that the men in the elevator continued to be unaware. He pulled his cell phone from his pocket and began typing away with his thumbs. If what she could make out from her glimpse was accurate, he'd just ordered a car service. Message sent, Evan replaced his phone with one hand and the other he casually slipped behind her. It was all she could do to keep her expression blank when that big warm hand scooped over her ass and squeezed.

When the doors opened, the other men filed out without looking back and Evan rumbled, "You may put your shoes on only till we reach the car." Z's whispered response was barely audible as she stepped back into her shoes. Evan clasped her arm just above her elbow and walked her off the elevator and out of the building without saying another word.

There was a town car, black and shiny, waiting right in front of the building and as soon as the driver spotted them he jumped out to open the back door. Evan helped her in and before she could slide across the bench seat, his hands cupped her armpits and laid her back. The door had barely closed behind him when the car started moving. Ziporah registered that there was privacy glass between them and the driver but she was so turned on she didn't think it would matter if it wasn't there.

"Hands up, sugar," Evan ordered in a growl. "I want those hands on your breasts." Z jolted in shock, sure he had been about to tell her to grasp the seat or the door, but never herself. "Do as I say. Unbutton that blouse and let me see you touch those pretty little things for me. That's it," he said as she shakily obeyed his bidding. "There you go, that's the way. Such a pretty little bra. Open it. Ah, so very lovely, now play with them."

Ziporah had never understood the appeal of doing this. Playing with herself, when there was a man right here in front of her to do it for her. Why would any woman choose that? For that matter, why would a man? If he had a willing woman right in front of him, why wouldn't he want his own hands on her?

Now she got it. There was something so incredibly sexy about watching him as he watched while her fingers squeezed and plucked and tickled on her own small breasts. Evan looked enthralled, and it made her feel powerful and enchanting.

"Don't stop. Don't you dare stop," Evan demanded as his hands went to her dress slacks and he yanked them from her body. His eyes never left her busy fingers as he lowered his head and devoured her. She bucked and cried out at the suction and his talented tongue brought her to a fast, hard climax in record time.

He wasn't through, wasn't through by a long shot from the looks of it. Those massive shoulders bunched as his arms wrapped around her hips and he lifted her lower body clear off the seat and growled, "Again," without lifting his mouth from her still pulsing clit. He sucked and lapped and gorged himself until a second, harder climax poured across his lips. He had one foot braced on the floor and one knee on the seat, while her legs were draped over his shoulders. As Ziporah jerked and gasped, the sight of him and how he looked right then was a visual delight that only added to her mind-blowing pleasure. And still he watched, so she continued to torment her nipples for him.

With one hand, Evan freed himself from his slacks, then gripped her hips with bruising force and slammed into her. They both cried out at the impact and froze for one endless moment where even the world seemed to hold its breath for them.

Finally, Evan could hold back no longer and he thundered into her with powerful lunges of his hips that rocked her entire being. And Ziporah countered every hard thrust, beat for beat. They went at each other like animals, and at a pace like that, it couldn't last. When she came with a scream that she muffled by biting the leather upholstery, five earth-shattering thrusts later, Evan followed with a grunt and a shudder that shook his entire body.

"Best damn lunch I ever had." All Ziporah could do was nod, wide-eyed and panting, in agreement.

Chapter Twenty-Four

In the weeks that followed, the three of them became inseparable. The flirting texts, the stolen lunches, and evenings spent in wild, abandoned passion. The fall was holding tight, with riotous colors and Halloween and Thanksgiving decorations everywhere, but for the first time in seven years, Cami was not lost to the darkness. It cropped up sometimes and brought a sadness to her that she tried to hide, but both Z and Cami agreed that this was the easiest fall season she'd ever had.

Evan and Ziporah spent most nights at the Tavern with Cami. There was a comfortable couch against the wall, away from most of the noise, which the two of them had commandeered as their own. Evan with his laptop, would pound away at the keys, compiling pie charts and comparison grids and things that were way beyond what either woman could comprehend. Z was just as bad, with her case files and her briefcase, scribbling away as she jotted down notes and muttered incessantly.

They loved it there, not only did being there allow them to be close to the third of their triad, but Cami had made the place live up to its name. It truly was a haven from the chaos of the outside world. Without fail, the music was never too loud and always fit the mood. Most of the people that were drawn there were fun-loving, inviting and all-around good company. The drinks were never watered down, and the food was worth fighting over. Word had gotten out of Natacha's cheesecake and even Evan was addicted. The feisty cook had warmed to him eventually and started setting aside a slice for him if she knew he was coming in.

Cami sang almost constantly. Her voice would ring out in perfect harmony from wherever she was in the tavern. She could be behind the bar filling a drink order and a song would catch her fancy, so she'd start singing along. Or cleaning the tables during open mic night, when someone would fumble or their confidence would desert them and she would join right in, adding her voice to theirs to bolster them up and help get them through.

It did not escape Cami's notice that every time she sang, Evan stopped what he was doing and listened. It thrilled her that he liked her voice, and filled her with a pleasure she had a hard time naming. That something she could do would stop a man like him in his tracks was a heady thing.

The tavern was closed for the night and the three of them were alone as Cami was doing inventory for tomorrow's order while Evan and Z were still working away on their own tasks. All three of them had important work to do; duties that responsible adults knew had to be fulfilled. So, to Cami's way of thinking, it was the perfect time to play.

With her clipboard in hand, she strolled along the inside of the bar seemingly taking notes on which bottles were low and needed to be replaced. As though without even noticing that she was doing it, Cami opened up her mouth and started singing.

It was intended to be an upbeat number but Cami sang slow and sultry; it was a song about sex, and she made sure to put plenty of gravel in the low notes and breathe in the high ones.

She tried to appear as though she wasn't enticing him on purpose while she cooed about what a bad girl she was, but Cami had never been one for subterfuge, so she was sure she failed miserably. When she sang about liking the smell of sex, she thought if she was any more turned on, she'd start glowing.

When she peeked to see what effect her song was having on Evan, she was smugly pleased to see that, like always, he'd stopped what he was doing and was watching her. "Sticks and stones may break my bones, but chains and whips excite me."

He didn't take his eyes off of her as he set his computer to the side, reached one hand into his fly, and cupped Z by the back of the head with his other. Cami's voice almost faltered when he urged the other woman to her knees between his spread legs and lowered her head. The lyrics for the next verse were beyond her comprehension at that point so she sang a jumble of rumbly vocal riffs that sounded like sex put to rhythm until she got to the chorus."

All the while, that stare, that beautiful emerald stare never left Cami's face as she sang to him about sex and love and longing.

It was hard to keep her voice steady and remember what line was next as Cami watched Z going down on him. She couldn't see anything other than her friend's silky brown hair bobbing up and down, but she didn't need to. It was hot and erotic and tantalizing.

The song was coming to an end when Evan lifted one hand to crook his finger at her, while his other hand continued to hold Z in place. Cami started forward, careful not to rush, she tried to look sensual and worldly instead of eager. She put sway in her body that Evan noticed as his eyes coursed up and down as her steps drew her closer. She timed it so the last note still hanging in the air by the time she made it to his side.

"Remove your shoes." Ah, that's why Z had dropped to do his bidding without her usual token resistance, Cami thought, she'd been barefoot already. Cami would've liked to have been wearing high heels or stilettos so she could kick them off with a sexy flounce, but as her luck would have it, she was in cowboy boots and they were a bitch.

She had to plop her bottom on the floor and yank and tug to get the stubborn things off. Cami didn't mind though, Z hadn't stopped what she was doing and Evan had continued to stare at her like she was Aphrodite, in spite of the fact that she was in a fight with her footwear.

"Come here." Evan reached a hand out to her and widened his legs as soon as the last boot hit the floor. Cami crawled forward eagerly and Z made room for her. This was new for them, going down on him at the same time. They had each done this for him before over these last weeks, but never together.

Z tilted her head to the side and her lips slid down that long column of flesh, so Cami leaned forward and wrapped hers around the bulbous head. The sound Evan made was a deep guttural growl and it lit a fire inside of her. She sucked and swirled her tongue as she braced one hand on Z's shoulder and reached out the other to cup and fondle his sack. When her friend came up, Cami turned her own head to the side so Z could have a turn at nuzzling that fat crest and slid her lips down the shaft this time.

They went back and forth like that for a long while, trading who got to pleasure the shaft with who got to pleasure the head, while both of them ran their hands over him constantly. Evan had excellent control, but everyone had a breaking point and he was fast approaching his.

Cami trembled as he fisted a hand in each of their hair and he brought them both to the sides of his cock so their noses were bumping and their lips were meshing together around him. He held them there like that as he groaned and his hips started to thrust between their sucking, drooling mouths. "Fuck! Oh girls, so fucking good. Christ Almighty, so fucking good." Then, with every muscle locked, his shouts rang out in the room as Evan came in a rush of heat that splashed in white hot streams over them both. Cami felt a hot trail coursing down her cheek and saw an identical one on Z's; more erupted from him as the two of them continued to lick and suck and moan.

Chapter Twenty-Five

Two nights later, Evan tripped on a landmine. He was at the girls' apartment and Ziporah was making dinner while he was in the living room with his brat. Cami was playful tonight, he was pleased to see. She'd been more and more playful and bratty the longer they were together and he loved to see her blossoming like this. The polite and soft-spoken shy little girl was a distant memory; in her place was a sweet brat that he found irresistible. She was currently hiding the remote behind her back and refusing to change the channel from her ridiculous vampire show.

"I'm not gonna tell you again, brat," Evan said with his hands braced on the back of the couch. He'd chased her around it three times already and though her giggles filled his heart with joy, enough was enough. "I'm watching football and that's the end of it. Now hand over the remote." Her lips parted and he could see her remember at the last minute not to stick out her tongue. "Yeah, you know what will happen if you poke that thing out at me." She smiled big and bright and more of that heartwarming laugh flowed forth.

"I bet you wish I would," she taunted, her little tail end shaking back and forth to add emphasis to her already sassy words. "But you're not gonna get that lucky tonight. And we wanna watch Buffy. So no, Sir. Take that." With a mock roar, Evan bolted over the back of the couch and was after her. She turned with a delightful squeal to run for the hall and Evan reached out to grasp her by the arm. His aim was just a hair off and what he caught was the edge of her blouse instead. The thin material gave with a resounding rip.

The world turned upside down in the flash of a moment. His playful, sweet, innocent brat went cold with terror and her giggling squeals turned into the torturous screams of the damned. Dimly, he heard a surprised shout from the kitchen and the clang of pots hitting the floor from Z, as Cami swung out in blind fury and backpedaled into a wall.

Evan reached for her with both arms, trying to draw her in so he could calm her down but that only seemed to make it worse. Her body arched back violently in an effort to escape him and the crack of her head hitting the plaster was as loud as a gunshot. Evan's gut turned to a cold, hard ball of ice.

Ziporah was there now, so even though it was the last thing he wanted to do, Evan opened his arms and stepped back.

"Shhh, it's okay baby. Shhh now, it's okay. I'm here, I got you. Shhh." Both women were crying as Z eased them to the floor. Cami lay flat on her back with her head and shoulders cradled in Z's arms as her body jerked like she was having seizures. Evan wanted to kill someone once Cami started talking. All Cami could say was, "He hurt me. He hurt me, Z. He hurt me."

"I know baby," Z whispered, cupping her friend's face and pressing it close to her own heaving chest. "I know he did. But it's over. That was a long time ago. Come back to us now, Cam. Come back to me."

Evan crouched down and braced his elbows on his knees. He watched helplessly as the two women flailed in the trauma of their past. He didn't dare touch either of them while in the grips of this flashback and though necessary, the restraint was a wound on his heart.

His legs had started to go numb when Cami finally passed the worst of it and curled into a ball on her side around Ziporah. "Okay, there she is. There's my girl." Z tightened her hold on Cami and kissed her repeatedly. On her head and cheek and temple, wherever she could reach. "There you are, my sweet Cam." With one last kiss to Cami's sweat dampened hair, Z nuzzled her cheek against the matted curls and turned to look at Evan.

Those fierce and confident brown eyes that could level entire courtrooms were haunted and drenched. The pain there, the anguish was every bit as crippling a blow as Cami's. Both of the women before him were survivors, although from the way this scene had played out, only one of them had suffered an attack.

Even though he couldn't touch them, Evan refused to leave their sides until this had passed. Eventually Cami gave a watery sniffle and peeked out at him from Z's arms. When she saw him there waiting, her face told him everything. That expression said 'I'm sorry', 'it's not your fault', 'please forgive me', and it made him crazed.

"I can see what you want to say." It took a Herculean effort to keep his voice gentle, when all he wanted to do was shout. "And I'm begging you–don't. Don't say one word of apology to me. That doesn't belong here, not for this. Not ever." She nodded at him and her face crumpled anew as fresh tears fell.

"You ready to get up now?" Ziporah gave a last squeeze to Cami and then briskly rubbed her back. "Let's go wash up. Come on, I'll help you." The two women staggered to their feet and stumbled down the hall like they'd spent the night drinking.

Only then did Evan shove to his feet and walk away. Needing to do something, anything, to keep from breaking everything in the house out of frustrated fury, he marched into the kitchen to see what he could do there. He'd heard things dropping earlier, so there was bound to be something in here for him to keep his mind occupied until they came back.

What hadn't fallen to the floor, had been left on the stove to burn. So Evan threw all of it away and took his aggression out by scrubbing the pots and pans. Unfortunately, the chore didn't take up enough time or enough of his thoughts.

He wanted to ram his fool head into the walls until he knocked some sense into it. Why hadn't he asked them? Why hadn't he delved into the pain and vulnerability that they both wore so clearly? Evan scrubbed hard enough at the pan in his hands that he was scratching it with the iron wool mesh as he berated himself for what he considered unforgivable negligence.

It was the same with the birth control and medicals. He'd been so turned inside out and upside down by his desire–no, his need– to have them, that he'd taken a risk he'd *never* taken before in his life. Evan had let the pleasure and the joy that they brought to him cloud his judgment and his lack of action had brought them to this night. The memory of their pain weighed on his heart like a cancer and Evan could only blame himself. There was a part of his brain trying to argue that this trauma wasn't his doing, but the truth in his eyes was that he should have known. That if he'd only talked to them, delved into their pasts, then this whole sorry mess could have been avoided.

With a snarl, Evan ordered food to be delivered, he had no idea what kind of food the girls would be in the mood for after something like this, so he ordered from three different places and enough to feed an army. He might not be able to go back and keep this from happening tonight, but he damn well promised himself that he was going to do everything in his power to insure that neither of them would have to suffer through another like this again. Not if he could help it.

With a smorgasbord of food spread out on the coffee and end tables, Evan heard the tale that had changed their lives forever. He refused to keep his hands to himself once they had come back in the room. They were his and no ghost from the past was going to come between him and the women that belonged to him. So he sat in the center of the couch with each of them tucked under his arms and their legs draped over his.

"Oh my God, Evan," Ziporah said after a while with a shake of her head and a sad laugh that was nothing like the laugh he normally heard from her. "Look at all this food. There's no way we can eat all this."

"It was really sweet of you though," Cami offered in a shy watery whisper. "I can't believe you ordered so much just because I was upset." Evan squeezed them both a little tighter and gave them each a soft kiss on their temples.

"It was the only thing I could think to do," he told them. "Let's just eat what we want and the rest we'll drop off at a shelter."

So they did. The girls ate French fries with chow mein and spaghetti marinara with Philly cheese steak sandwiches. Nibbling and munching as the night wore on and as they did, they filled in the details of the attack and the events that followed.

Much later, after the girls had talked themselves out and eaten until they swore they were going to burst, Evan was in the kitchen dealing with the leftovers. "You don't have to do all this yourself." Ziporah's weary voice sounded just behind him and Evan turned to face her. "Let me help. She'll be fine. This was a bad one but we got her through okay." Evan leaned back against the counter and crossed his arms over his chest as he studied her for a moment.

"What do you mean we got *her* through it?" Evan wanted to know.

"Her flashback. It was a bad one but at least it was over relatively quickly."

Evan took two slow deep breaths before he could speak. It astounded him that she thought this flashback, the pain, was all on Cami's part. "Sugar, I know Cami gets help for dealing with what happened but have you ever gotten help for it?"

The baffled look on her face was all the answer he needed and on a soft curse Evan opened his arms and pulled her tight against his chest. "Oh, Ziporah. Your innocence was shattered that night right along with Cami's. That was the night you both found out monsters were real. Where was your family when this happened? You were there to take care of Cami. But who was there to take care of you? Didn't anyone see that this tore you up same as it did her?"

His words seemed to sink in and reach inside her. She didn't say a word to him but her arms cinched tight around his waist, she tucked her face in his neck and quite simply fell apart. She sobbed with silent, heart-rending grief that shook her entire body, and Evan's heart broke even more.

That no one had been there for her was another tragedy on top of an already tragic situation. He knew that she was the strong one, the one to always appear confident and unruffled, so he could understand how she had fooled so many and hid the devastation within her. But that didn't make it okay. All he could do now was hold her as she cried and promise himself that as long as she would let him, she would never have to be the strong one again.

It was an effort to keep up a calm front for their sake. On the inside, a murderous rage was boiling within him. That night, as the two of them slept, each curled tight against him in trusting slumber, Evan lay awake in torment.

Chapter Twenty-Six

It been more than a week since that fateful night, and Evan hadn't made love to them since. He wanted to give them time to heal, and if he were honest, time for himself to come to terms with it. That some asshole had done what he did to sweet innocent Cami brought tremors of rage to his hands every time the thought crossed his mind.

She deserved better than to have him touch her while he was still processing and dealing. It was only right that he wait, until nothing of what he now knew could taint their lovemaking. So, tonight he felt he could at least put it behind him and bury it. It would be there always, the helpless rage that he hadn't been there to protect her when she'd needed him, but he felt he was at a place where he could touch her without her seeing it.

"All right now, ladies." Evan raised his voice so that it carried back to where the two were still fussing with themselves and their mirrors. "Come on out here and let's get finished so we can go. I ain't about to be late." There was a big dinner party at Cade's place.

Z came out first and the sight of her stirred his blood. She had on a deep purple dress that was probably called passionate orchid or something to that effect, all he knew was the color suited her perfectly. It was made of a soft-looking fabric that was thick and warm, with long sleeves and a skirt that flared out around her knees as she walked. It hung lovingly to her athletic form and showcased her slender build stupendously.

"Beautiful, sugar." Evan walked over and kissed her gently on her juicy painted lips. He wanted to stroke her silky hair but he didn't dare, as she had it piled up in one of those buns that look like a sexy mess with little bits dangling around her face. "In that color, I should call you sugarplum. You are stunning." She blushed and smiled and her skirt swayed around her knees as she rocked back and forth in pleasure at his complement.

"Cami is the slowest person on the planet," she told him in warning. "I kind of feel sorry for you, because you are never going to be on time for anything ever again." But then she smiled at him. "Only kinda sorry though, because now I'm not suffering alone."

"Oh yeah?" Evan headed toward the hall. "We will just see about that." He opened the door to Cami's room, ready to drag her out no matter what state she was in, but the sight before him froze him to the spot.

Cami had chosen one of those long-sleeved wraparound dresses in black for tonight. It cut low between her amazing breasts, parted high up her thigh and tied at her waist. The material was slinky and moved sinuously around her with her motions when she turned to face him. Evan tried, but he could see no indication of any undergarments and the spit dried up in his mouth. All those blonde, honeyed curls had been straightened and brought into submission in a tail that gathered at her neck and poured down her back. There was a small part in it, far off to the side just above her left temple that brought attention to her perfectly arched brows and the gleaming jewels of her eyes. Those lips that could tempt a saint were painted a deep shiny red and the beauty of her about brought him to his knees.

"I have no words." Evan walked to her with his hands turned up in a gesture of surrender. "There are no words for how beautiful you look right now." A blush warmed her cheeks and made her even more appealing, as Evan took her by the hand and led her out of the room. These two women, who were so different in both looks and personality, appealed to him on every level he had. Talk about your cup over flowing, Evan thought.

"I've got a surprise for you girls." They stood side-by-side in the middle of the living room and tried to look like the idea of a present didn't thrill them. Evan hid his smirk, because he knew his surprise wasn't going to be what they were expecting.

Reaching into his jacket pocket Evan pulled out a small egg-shaped toy and turned to Cami first. He knelt before her. "Open your legs for me. Come on, widen your stance. Wider." She obeyed with a curious and eager smile. "Now lift your skirt. Higher, get it out of my way." Once she did, Evan saw he'd guessed wrong, she was wearing panties. It was a miniscule thong made up of a couple of strips of lace and a tiny triangle of black satin. He moved that so-called barrier out of his way and swirled the egg over the lips now revealed. She was as beautiful down here as she was everywhere else. The delicate folds of skin, pink and glistening as he caressed them, were like an exotic flower. Arousal brought a dark rosy flush to them and he could hear her breath already getting choppy. He played for a moment, nudging her clitoris and stroking in and out, before placing a hand on her hip and pushing the vibrating toy deep inside. When she cried out for him and clutched at his shoulders, Evan leaned forward and kissed her right on her mound, drinking in the perfume of her arousal like the sweetest of wines. It took all his will power to stop himself from staying exactly where he was for the rest of the night.

Then he turned to Ziporah. "All right, your turn. You know what to do." She was wearing a thong, too; hers was white lace with a purple ribbon and a cute little bow. As he eased the panties aside, he pondered how they were different here, too. Z's skin tone was darker and her fragrance was all her own, yet every bit as enticing as Cami's. Evan pulled a matching egg out of his other pocket and repeated the same motions on her. When Ziporah became aroused, the lips plumped up and became ultra sensitive, begging for the stroke of his tongue. Denying himself the pleasure of exploring them was no small test of his control. He consoled himself with the promise of the coming night and teased the small vibrator in and out and rubbed it over her clit until her slender hips were following his motions and her pussy was glistening wet. He was so hard, he could hammer nails with his shaft.

"Okay, rules for this evening." Evan stood in front of them and felt his chest swell at the site before him. His ladies were stunning, and so turned on he could practically see the arousal coming off them like heat waves of the pavement. He smiled at them then held up two innocent looking devices, one in each hand. They could easily be mistaken for remotes to unlock a car or disable its alarm, but considering what just transpired and what lay deep within each woman's pussy, they knew exactly what he held. "I am going to turn these on whenever I damn well please." Then he tucked one in each pocket and turned toward the door. As expected, they burst out laughing.

"That's it?" Of course it was Cami, his sweet brat, who was going to poke at him first. "You stand here and say we're going to discuss the *rules,* but then the only thing you have to say is that?" He turned on her remote. Her squeak was like foreplay to his ears.

"Yep." Then he shrugged into his leather jacket and turned for the door. Both girls continued to laugh, even as they joined him.

It was going to be a fun night. They were ready for this step. Cami and Z had been the ones to approach him about the club. He loved scening in public, but both his girls were new to the lifestyle, so he was content to play in private for as long as they needed. When they had timidly brought up the subject of playing with the others, they'd talked over every concern the girls had and then he'd made the calls to put this night in motion. As their laughter continued to bubble around them on their way to the elevators, Evan felt their eagerness and anticipation of the coming night as clearly as he felt his own and it was as potent as a shot of whisky.

Chapter Twenty-Seven

Cade Marshall owned an exclusive nightclub that catered to the elite of New York City. The restaurant adjacent to the club had the longest reservation waiting list of any place in town. The private rooms in the back of the club were exclusively member-only and it was the most well equipped BDSM establishment that Evan had ever seen.

The evening had started with a five-course gourmet meal that had Evan's girls moaning with each bite. He could hardly blame them, the food was that good. All throughout the meal, Evan tormented his ladies with their toys, turning them on in the middle of a sentence or turning them up, just when one of them would take a drink. They were flustered and off center, just how he liked it.

Sitting around the table with Cade, Trevor and Riley, plus Brice and Terryn along with Gage and Zoe had truly been a blast. All of them shared the alternative lifestyle. Cade and Trevor were married to Riley, and the three of them lived happily as an unconventional married unit. Riley had just given birth to her second child a little over a year ago and they were already talking about adding a third. The kids were tucked away in a suite with Riley's parents for the night. Evan thought it was hilarious that the men chuckled at Riley for her nonstop texts to check on them, even as they did the same thing when they thought she wasn't looking. The love and passion between the three of them was undeniable and considering Evan's current situation, it was also an inspiration that planted a seed of hope in his heart.

Brice and Terryn, as well as Zoe and Gage were also in Dom/sub relationships, and so the conversation was unguarded and lively. Evan's trained eye told him that his subs were not the only ones wearing equipment tonight. From the looks of things, all the subs were. And didn't that just make things fun.

"What I wanna know is," Terryn asked the table at large, "when Evan knew he was a Dom. I know everybody else's story but yours."

"Ooh," his Cami squealed in agreement, "yeah, I want to hear this one, too. How old were you when you figured it out?" She looked at him with her big blue eyes widened in curious enjoyment and denying her never even crossed his mind.

"I was about six, I think." As expected the entire table erupted in laughter.

"Oh my god, please tell me you are joking." Ziporah, his beautiful dark haired angel, laughed as she reached over and put her hand on his leg. Evan felt his chest expand with the familiar warmth he felt every time she touched him and he clasped his hand over hers to keep it there. Wanting nothing in the world more than for both of his women to never stop touching him.

"Nope, serious as a heart attack," he told her with a shake of his head. "I didn't know that it was a BDSM thing until much later but, yeah, I think six is about right."

"So what was it that triggered this knowledge then?" Brice wanted to know.

"Dudley Do Right." He had to wait for the laughs to die down before he could continue.

"What is that?" Zoe asked, baffled by the laughs around her.

"It's a cartoon from before your time," Gage told her with a rueful shake of his head. "Infant." More laughter followed. Gage was more than a decade older than his young bride, and though the two were deliriously in love, the age difference was a startling adjustment for her family, not to mention for Gage, who had resisted mightily when she had set out to seduce him.

"To be a bit more specific," Evan continued, "it was Dastardly Dan." More laughter, Evan even chuckled as Cami's giggles bubbled forth nonstop. "See, he kept tying Penelope Pitstop up in ropes and leaving her on train tracks. I was fascinated. I used to root for poor Dan and get so miffed every time all his pretty ropes came off. I never understood why I liked seeing her tied up like that, but on the playground at school, I was known as the double D. As for when I connected the dots and tried it in real life? I was twenty-two the first time I joined a BDSM club." He smiled and winked at his ladies before he added, "And I registered under the name of Dan." Laughter was as plentiful and rich as the food and both were lingered over.

Cami and Ziporah were not the only ones who kept jumping in their seats and shooting glares at their man, either. Evan thought it was funny as hell, sexy too. As the night wore on all five women became flushed and breathless. And all the men, himself included, lost more and more of their civilized veneer along the way.

By the time the party moved to the dance floor, the mood was no longer playful but hungry. Cade and Trevor were the first to cave. Not one for sharing their treasure, they only danced a few songs before the need to have Riley naked overrode everything else. It was no surprise to anyone when Cade and Trevor each manacled a hand around her wrists and marched her to the private elevator. It led to their penthouse on the top floor of the building, where they lived.

Brice and Terryn were the next to go. The two of them slipped back toward the private rooms within moments of the first three's departure, with Brice's hand tangled in his redhead's fiery locks.

That left Gage and Zoe with the three of them. Evan didn't usually dance, unless it was to country music, so he was sitting at a table watching Gage get his groove on with all three of their women. The man was as big as a mountain and yet he moved like Fred Astaire. He twirled and swirled, lifted and dipped all three women without ever missing a step. It was a sight to behold.

The club was an edgy one, filled with people who knew there were no-holds barred and they were safe to act as they desired, so the mood had a sexually greedy undertone. The music was pulsing like the throb of an aroused cock and the dancers on the floor moved free of inhibitions or worries of judgments.

Across the sea of swaying thrusting bodies, Evan and Gage made eye contact, and the signal was clear. It was time. Evan hit the switch on high for each of the girls' toys, just as Gage wrapped an arm around Zoe and motioned for them to follow. As soon as Gage and the women got to the table, Evan swiped his credit card through the mechanism in the middle of it. The table he had chosen came with the privacy option. From the floor rose a Plexiglas half-circle around them that sealed them off from the rest of the room. With a wall at their backs and a half-circle of glass surrounding them, the sudden quiet was almost jarring. As soon as the hollow glass reached the ceiling it filled with a swirling mist and colored lights. It didn't offer complete privacy, the mist was in constant motion that allowed glimpses in and out, and Evan figured it was the perfect test to see how his ladies responded to exhibition.

"Wow." Cami's voice was delighted and she rushed over to touch and explore, while Z just watched him with an expectant expression on her face.

"The question I gotta ask," Gage said, his accent thicker with arousal, "is are we gonna do this on the table or against the glass?"

"Why not both?" Evan retorted, and dragged Z up against his body and kissed her like it was the first time. His hand reach under her skirt, and his fingers arrowed into her to remove the egg that he'd used to drive her insane tonight. Once he got it out, he had enough brain cells left to remember to put it in his pocket rather than let it drop to the floor.

Then he reached out blindly with his free hand for Cami. She came to him with a whimper as he cupped her on the back of her head and brought her mouth to where he was still kissing Ziporah. He pressed the women's cheeks close together and kissed them both at the same time, all three tongues tangling and lapping as breaths and sighs mingled.

"Oh, darlin'," Evan heard Gage say, "I got a mind to make this fast and hard, so I can get you home and then do it long and slow." Evan pulled back from the kiss and using his grip on Cami, turned her and urged her to bend over the table. Once she was there his hands slipped up between her thighs and he retrieved her toy after first playing and probing, until she cried out for him. She was gasping by the time he was done and Evan knew it was just as much from watching Gage thundering into his wife against the Plexiglas as it was from him playing with her.

The table wasn't as tall as a hightop and Evan gauged that it was about perfect for what he had in mind. Cami was already bent over and spread out before him, her skirt flipped up out of the way and that juicy plump ass begging for a good pounding. "C'mere, sugar." Evan gripped Ziporah around her waist and lifted her onto the table over Cami. He helped her adjust on hands and knees, shifting and moving her until her weight was braced so that she wouldn't crush the other woman and her ass was lined up right on top of Cami's.

"Now there's a pretty sight," Gage said, having picked up Zoe and flipped her around. She was now bent over the other side of the table, watching the three of them as her Dom positioned himself behind her.

"You should see it from my view," Evan replied reverently. His hands were playing in the flesh he had lined up for his pleasure, making sure each woman was primed and ready for this. "Ladies, I need to hear your safe word," he told them as a signal to let them know it was on and there was no going back from here.

"T – T Rex." Ziporah's voice was tremulous and aroused.

"T Rex." Cami's voice was equally aroused but there was a recklessness to it, a wild note that let him know having Gage and Zoe there was working for her. Big time.

Ziporah was in the perfect position for him when he stood to his full height, with Cami he had to bend his knees in order to reach her. So that's what he did first, with one hand on Cami's hip, he used his other to position his cock and slid inside his sweet brat with a groan. Once he was flush against that pillowy ass, he used his free hand to slide and play in Z's dripping cunt.

He plunged in and out of Cami's sweet pussy with his shaft, while he did the same to Ziporah's with his fingers. As Cami soaked his lap in her juices Ziporah soaked his hand and the aroma of them was intoxicating. The feel, the smell, the taste of these two women had become the baseline of his life. Fucking them, talking with them, just being with them and breathing the same air had become vital to his survival.

As the mist and colors that flashed in the glass surrounding them illuminated the scene, Evan came to startling revelation. *He loved them.* He loved everything about them. He loved Cami's creative and artistic heart just as much as he loved Ziporah's honorable and driven one. Their bodies, their minds, their flaws and their quirks, all of that and more combined to enslave him. As the beautiful truth of that settled into his soul with certainty, it brought him something he had not expected. It brought him peace.

Evan pulled out of Cami just as her first orgasm finished tearing through her walls and shifted to slam into Z. That first hard thrust sent Z catapulting into her own climax, and Evan had to freeze and grit his teeth to keep from joining her. Once the rhythmic clutching of her cunt had passed, he started thrusting hard and fast while he slipped a hand underneath to play with Cami.

"Never want to stop ladies," Evan told them fervently. "Never going to stop. You're mine." Evan reached out his free hand to fist Z's hair and pulled her head back in an arch. "You hear that, sugar? You're mine. You both are, you belong to me."

"Yes!" Ziporah screamed as another climax erupted within her.

"And I'm never–" Evan gave her one last hard thrust then pulled out and slammed into Cami. "Ever–" Out again and back into Z. "Going to–" Once more with a brutal thrust, he was back inside Cami. "Let. You. Go." With a sound that was unlike any he had ever made before, Evan pulled out, fisted himself and detonated. He watched as he stroked, and each fiery pulse of his release was a brand that splashed in white hot rivulets on the still quivering asses of the women he loved. It thrilled a deep primal part of him to mark them so carnally, each stream an insignia of ownership and a declaration of devotion.

Even the guttural shouts of Gage coming and the delighted squeals of Zoe following close on his heels didn't draw his attention from his ladies. In this moment, he didn't think anything short of World War III would have managed to do that.

Chapter Twenty-Eight

"Z, I think we need to talk." Cami was dressed in her favorite lounge around the house lazy clothes, which consisted of her sweatpants that said juicy on the butt, a sports bra and a baggy ancient sweatshirt. From her seat curled up on the couch, she faced her best friend with a ball of fear lodged in her throat.

"Sure honey." Ziporah answered and turned off the television before setting the remote back down and turning to face her. "What is it? What you need?" Cami smiled a little. That was Z, Cami said she had a need and Z was there to fill it. That was a street that went both ways and they both knew it, but at times like this, it still had the power to choke her up and bring tears to her eyes.

"It's Evan," Cami began, "I think we need to talk about Evan and the three of us." Z was nodding, and Cami wasn't even surprised to see that, as usual they were on the same page. "This is bigger and, I don't know, more I guess is the word I would use, than I thought it was going to be. This was supposed to be a fling. A couple of fun sessions with a hot Dom to break me in and get me started." Cami felt her eyes well up with tears as she looked Ziporah head-on and confessed." But it's more, it's so much more, Z. I think I love him."

"Oh, Cami." Ziporah's eyes filled with tears too, and the two of them reached toward each other and held hands across the cushion that separated them. "I think I knew that already." Her voice dropped to a whisper and her bottom lip quivered. "I think I was afraid of that, because I do, too." Cami felt her shoulders wilt in relief.

"Oh thank God!" Cami gushed as her fears melted away.

"What you mean? I was afraid you'd be mad." Z looked more than a little confused.

"Mad? Why on earth would I be mad?" Cami asked truly baffled. "This is perfect."

"Perfect? How can you say that? We're both in love with the same man." Z sounded incredulous now.

"Don't you see? Now we can all stay together, we can be like this forever. We can make this work, we won't have to ever be apart. Don't you want that? Hasn't this been better than we ever thought it would be?"

"Yes, yes it has. But can we do this for the long haul? What about marriage? And what about kids? We both want kids. How are we going to do this? Really, how could we possibly make this work?"

Cami scooted closer until she could wrap her arms around Z and hold her tight. She didn't have all the answers, and she wasn't going to pretend like she did, or like this was going to be easy. But she knew if the two of them stuck together, they always got what they wanted. And, thank God, they both wanted Evan. So, she hoped for his sake he loved them back, because they were keeping him. "I don't know, sugar," Cami teased, using Evan's pet name for her, "but we can make it work. If Cade, Trevor and Riley can make it work, then so can we."

"So, how are we going to break the news to Evan that he's stuck with us? You wanna tie him up in the sex cave and not let them out until he agrees to let us keep him?" Cami laughed at the ornery note in Z's voice.

"See?" Cami said with a chuckle." This is why I don't understand how come I'm the brat and you're the sugar."

Chapter Twenty-Nine

"So you see, that's how Pac-West Distributions is really the only choice for you to make." Evan watched as Mark smiled and spread his hands with a slight tilt of his head, while the board members clapped politely at the end of his presentation. He kept his applause to himself. There was nothing he could find wrong with this man's company or his offer, but Evan was still reluctant.

His reluctance stemmed from his own personal bias, though, so he didn't think he would be able to hold out much longer. The stockholders and the board members were really pushing for this merger and Evan's gut didn't hold a candle to the bottom line.

"That was a good show," Evan told the other man once the board members had filed out. "You have strong numbers, a good reputation and a solid marketing plan behind you."

"We do." Mark told him in a strong and confident voice. "I know there are two others still in the running and I just want to tell you our company is prepared to do what it takes to get this done. Tell you what, why don't you and I meet for drinks this weekend and talk it over? You can tell me what is keeping those other two in the running, and I'll tell you how I can deliver above and beyond them." Evan nodded reluctantly. "Sure. I'll text you the address to this little tavern I like and we can meet there on Friday night."

That evening after dinner, the three of them were at the girls' apartment. Evan was seated on the couch in his favorite position with Cami and Z tucked under each arm. Ziporah was riding pretty high at the moment. She had won a big case that was close to her heart and one more bad guy was off the streets. Her best friend, Cami, and she had never been closer, and she was in love with a handsome, successful, southern Dom. In her mind, life was just about perfect.

"So yeah," Ziporah finished with deep satisfaction, "he got fifteen years and he won't be eligible for parole for at least six. That's pretty good; that's more than I'd hoped for."

"Well, I'm proud of you," Evan said with sincerity in his voice. "You worked hard, you dug out the facts, and you pushed those witnesses to get their details straight. That DA is lucky to have you, and so are the people in this city." He leaned over and kissed her with simple undiluted affection. "And so am I."

"God, I love you." She hadn't meant to say that. But the feeling just filled her so much that if she didn't let the words out, she would burst. She didn't take her eyes off his face, so she had the pleasure of watching the truth of those words sink in and take root. The look on his face reassured and warmed her from head to toe.

"I'm in love with you, too." Evan's head whipped around and he stared at Cami while she looked back at him in complete seriousness. "We talked about this the other day." Z tried hard not to laugh as Cami's inner-brat came out to play. "We plotted for hours about how we would tie you up and torture you until you agreed to let us keep you."

"Oh ladies, my beautiful, sweet ladies." Z felt Evan's hand shake as he reached out and laid it gently on her cheek.

He did the same to Cami looking from one to the other of them with his heart and his eyes.

"You went and ruined all of my big plans. See, I was going to take you out on a little trip to see my spread back in Texas. Because, even though I'm up here for the long haul, Texas will always be my home and we'll be spending a lot of time there over the years."

Z felt joyous emotion gathering like a storm in her chest as she guessed where this was heading, and from the tears coursing down Cami's cheeks, she saw that she wasn't the only one who knew where this was going either.

"When I got you both there, I was going to take you out into the moonlight under the stars, because New York has a lot to offer, but it's got nothing on Texas when it comes to the night sky. Then, when I had you both there, drenched in moonlight highlighted by fireflies, I was going to tell you that I was in love with you. I was going to tell you that I wanted to marry you both. And I was going to ask you to do me the honor of spending your lives with me."

That storm inside Z broke. Tears poured forth hard and fast and as Evan gathered her close, she could hear the same thing happening with Cami. He loved them, it didn't make sense to the rest of the world and she knew it never would, but he loved them. For her and for Cami it made sense, though, and that was all they needed, really.

With the gentlest of kisses, Evan soothed away the tears. With two big palms, he cupped Ziporah's face and brought her up till they were nose to nose and he looked straight into her eyes with his burning gaze and told her, "I love you Ziporah. I love you so much it clouds my mind." Then as tears fell even faster, he kissed her like it was the first time and the last time.

Evan pulled back and laid a gentle kiss on her nose then turned to Cami next. One hand cupped her chin and the other he placed along her cheek. "Cami," he started, his accent rich and deep with his emotions, "my sweet, sweet brat. I love you. I love everything about you and I'm going to keep loving you till the day I die." Then, even as she burst out into full blown bawling, he sealed his mouth to hers and kissed her with all the passion he'd just shown Z.

He touched them both with reverent tenderness after that and built the passion with soft slow strokes of his hands and his tongue. Ziporah tilted her head back on a dreamy sigh as those warm lips coursed down her neck, while Cami whimpered with budding arousal when he turned and did the same to her.

With no rush at all, his hands brushed her clothing out of the way, piece by piece until she was naked. She was so lost in his lazy lovemaking that she wasn't even aware that he'd gotten her naked until she noticed he'd gotten Cami naked, too.

His touch was so confident and sure as he swept his hands over her body, that Z felt branded, marked as his. With insistent hands, he urged her to her back on the couch and lowered that beautiful head. He lapped softly at the flesh between her legs with that same slow tenderness and the effect was galvanizing. Evan lifted his head and Ziporah opened her eyes to watch as he turned his mouth to Cami next.

He had placed her sitting on the back of the couch, with her legs on either side of Z. The erotic view turned the fire within her into an inferno. She could clearly see Evan's chin working as he lapped and drank between the other woman's legs, and it was an incomparable thrill that while doing that, his hands never stopped moving on either of them.

That was one of the miracles of being with Evan; neither she nor Cami ever felt neglected or left out when the three of them were together. When they were alone, Cami and she often joked that the man was, in reality, Dionysus, the Greek god of sex. As Ziporah lay there watching him devour Cami while his hand was pumping between her own legs, she almost believed it.

Ziporah felt Evan crook his fingers up and change the direction of his thrust from in and out to up and down and her hands started scrambling. Faster he stroked, faster, while still lapping at Cami, and Ziporah felt that wonderful weight building and gathering force deep inside of her.

Z groaned, the climax so close that she was teetering on the edge and the sound spurred Evan on. With a growl, he plunged faster within her and sucked greedily at the pussy in his mouth, and Cami came at the same time she did. Both of them crying out while their bodies thrashed in the throes of their peak, and still Evan continued. Insatiable, starved for them both.

Ziporah was nearing peak again, and she could tell Cami was too when Evan pulled back with a growl. With impatient hands, he yanked his clothes from his body and sat on the middle cushion. His rumbled commands were barely discernible as he positioned Cami in a straddle over his lap facing him and pulled Z until she was sitting on his face with his head braced on the back of the couch. When that talented and amazing mouth went to work on her, Z leaned forward and nuzzled her head in the crook of Cami's neck and shoulder and felt Cami do the same to her. Evan's hips thundered into Cami, jolting her body in hard thrusts, while his mouth had Z's hips grinding against his face. And as he devoured them with mouth and cock, they clung to each other and came. Endlessly.

Z felt, as well as heard, Evan's shouted, *"Oh fuck!"* And then the body beneath them began to tremble and quake as he lost himself in his own magnificent climax that filled their whole world with light.

Z laughed like a drunk as she and Cami toppled to the side, where Cami then tumbled to the floor and Evan lay sprawled where they'd left him, destroyed.

"Oh my God, Z!" Cami said in mock horror, "I think we killed him." Z laughed then nudged Evan with her toes against his hip. "And that, Cami," Evan's smile was more than a little lopsided as he and Ziporah said in unison, "is why we call you the brat."

Chapter Thirty

Friday night at Haven was a happening time. The mood was lively, the food and drink were plentiful, and Cami was in love. All was right in her world. Her business was booming, her bank account was healthy, and so was her body. But the two best things about her life right now where the people she was in love with.

Cami was so euphoric and happy, for a full thirty seconds she didn't believe what her eyes were telling her she saw. Mark Wahlberg had just walked into her tavern. He looked exactly the same. Blond and charming, thick of build, with a boyish grin that used to make her heart flutter, but now made her skin crawl. She had no idea what to do. Cami had never prepared herself for this moment. Her skin was covered in an instant sheen of icy sweat and she felt as though she were paralyzed. Not one of her muscles would move. It was a living nightmare; she was frozen as he drew closer to the bar and inside her head was a distant roaring scream of denial.

She knew a lot of victims dreamed of facing their attackers one day. They had dreams of being able to say all the things that they never had the chance to say before. Some of them had hopes that their attackers would offer words of sorrow or remorse. But that wasn't Cami; she prayed to God that she would never have to see this man again. Yet the answer to that prayer was a big fat *NO* apparently, because as nonchalant as you please, her own personal bogeyman was making his way toward the bar.

The last time Mark had laid eyes on her, his had been drenched with remorse and tears as he begged her to forgive him. When he looked up and caught sight of her now, there was nothing contrite about the look he gave her. His face was filled with smug derision, and he even had the nerve to look her up and down as he leaned against the bar.

"Well, well, well." How could she have ever found the snake before her charming, Cami asked herself. "Should have known a little tease like you would end up a barfly." The glass in Cami's hand shattered to the floor at his callused words. "Careful doll, you're gonna get yourself fired. Even a rack like yours ain't worth losing money over."

Cami couldn't believe what she was hearing. His heartless words and sneering expression was the stuff of nightmares. What happened, she wondered, to everything being all a big tragic mistake? The man before her now hadn't a shred of regret.

The edges of her vision started to go black, and echoes of that night were ringing through her ears. Her screams, the sound of her clothes being ripped to tatters, the unconscionable thud that his fist made as it connected with her flesh. And worst of all, the angry snarling grunts as he'd raped her. It was closing in on her, obscuring her grasp on reality and unleashing years of frustration, fear and anguish.

"Get out." Her voice was unrecognizable even to her own ears. "Get out now and get out fast." If possible, his sneer became even more defined.

"All those years ago you ran me out of school because you were a little cock tease. You ain't running me out of anywhere ever again."

Everything went black. Cami didn't know how it happened, but from one heartbeat to the next, she went from behind the bar to on top of him. She didn't think, she couldn't see, she couldn't even feel anything. It was like those horrible nightmares where you're swinging as hard as you can, but your fists seem to be moving in slow motion and not making any impact at all. She was pounding with as much strength as she could summon, screaming as loud as her lungs would allow, and still it wasn't enough.

Evan vaulted from his seat in the back of the Tavern as soon as he heard that now familiar sound of Cami's scream. He rounded the bar and took in the scene in a millisecond. Cami was a woman possessed as she wailed and beat on the person beneath her. Evan raced forward to pick her up and was enraged to see the man he'd considered doing business with swing out with his fist at the woman he loved.

Even as he lifted Cami and began to pull her out of reach, Mark stood and lashed out with a leg that Evan deflected just in time. As that bruising kick connected with his own hip, Evan looked at Mark in furious shock.

Evan had already had Cami in his arms and was moving her away when Mark had come after them to kick at her. Evan didn't know what had happened to start this, but he did know that as soon as Cami was safe, he was gonna wipe the floor with the other man.

That's when all hell broke loose for a second time. Ziporah came rushing from the bathrooms with the screech of a banshee, leaped into the air from a good two feet away and took Mark down in a flying tackle. If Evan hadn't been so worried about the delicate frame of the other woman he loved, he would've been as impressed as hell with that move.

As it was, all he could think about was the fact that Mark had punched and tried to kick Cami, so there was no telling what he would do to Ziporah.

Thankfully, Natacha was there for him to hand Cami over to. He shoved her into the other woman's restraining arms, because Cami had rallied and was trying with all her might to dive back in.

When Evan turned back around, Mark and Ziporah had rolled until Mark was over her, with his fist raised and his other hand clamped on her slender neck. It didn't deter her a bit, Z's legs were scrambling and her fists were flying all the same. Before Mark's fist could land, Evan locked an arm around Mark's throat and yanked him off of his woman.

"I don't know who the fuck raised you," Evan snarled in the other man's ear as he wrenched a little tighter on that throat, cutting off the airways until he quit trying to get away, "but I can tell you they did a piss-poor job of it. What kind of a man would hit a woman?" Just asking the question left a sour taste in his mouth, so Evan spat on the floor right in front of him. "A worthless one."

With more force than was needed, because Mark must've realized who had a hold of him and was trying to make nice now, Evan drug him out the door and threw him to the sidewalk. "You'd best get your miserable ass out of here and never come back." Evan could only guess at what the other man saw on his face, because any angry retort or bullshit excuse dried up pretty damn fast. He just turned and jogged away, apparently so spooked he didn't think walking was fast enough.

When Evan went back inside, the place was still in chaos. People were riding high on the thrill of the fight. As he made his way to the back couch where Z and Cami were sitting with their arms around each other, he heard the same story being told by every cluster of people that he passed.

Evan crouched down in front of his two women and placed a hand on each of their cheeks. "How are my sugar and my brat, huh?" He tipped forward and kissed each sweat-dampened forehead. "Somebody wanna tell me what happened?"

"That was Mark Wahlberg," Cami said, as though she was stating a revelation.

"Yeah, I know who he was. My company was considering a partnership with his, but that's not going to be happening now." Evan saw the look come over Z's face that was boiling with intensity.

"Mark was the one, Evan," she said and knocked the wind out of him. "He was the one that raped Cami." Evan felt his entire body readying itself for battle, and as a blanket of rage settled upon him, he stood to his feet and headed for the door without a word.

He started out in a slow purposeful stride, but within five steps, he was running. Running because he remembered that bastard had been jogging when he'd left, and Evan wanted to catch him. Because when he did, he was going to kill him.

He ran full-out for about five blocks in a blind rage before the cold slapped some sense into him. With a curse at his own stupidity, Evan turned and got his ass back to his women. They didn't need him landing his fool-ass in jail, or to have to clean him up after a brawl. They needed him to be there for them, not the other way around. The sickening fury that threatened to choke him was his own issue to deal with, and not a priority. His women were his priority now and always, and he was an idiot for forgetting that for even a second. By the time he was back at the couch, they had pulled themselves together somewhat. Evan cursed himself again; he should have been here to help them recover from the shock, not out chasing that asshole in a testosterone-fuelled rage.

"So, since there's no blood, I'm assuming that means I won't have to put you in prison?" Ziporah asked with one eyebrow raised.

"Nah, sugar." Evan waved that away, and tried to give her a cocky grin despite the volcanic rage still boiling within him. "I didn't have to kill him. You and the wildcat here took care of that for me." Cami surprised the hell out of him when she laughed at that. "Oh, you think that's funny do you? You scared the bejesus out of me. I about had a heart attack when I heard you screaming, then came around and saw you grappling with him." Now that he'd managed to cool down a little, he was actually very impressed.

"I wish I could tell you I was sorry," Cami said, trying to keep a straight face and failing, "but that felt so good. So good to finally face him and hit him the way I wanted to for years." At that, her cute little nose wrinkled and she pouted at him. "It kind of sucked at the same time, too. Because I couldn't tell if I was hitting him or not. I couldn't feel anything." She held up hands that were swollen and puffy for him to see.

"Ah, slugger, look at your poor knuckles. These are going to be hurting tomorrow, and besides that, you broke two of your pretty nails." Evan clucked his tongue and kissed each swollen joint tenderly, as he cupped her sore hands in his palms. "Well brat, you may not have felt your blows landing, but from the looks of these he sure as hell did." She smiled at him with a mischievous grin that warmed his heart and turned him inside out.

"I sure did, huh?" Evan laughed and nodded, then leaned forward and kissed her smiling lips.

"And what about your hands, sugar?" Evan turned to the other woman of his life to inspect her for injuries. Anger surged anew when he saw bruises already forming on her throat. "God damn him."

"I'm sure he already has," Z informed him in a voice that was a little rough around the edges. "I just wish he would get on with the lightning bolts already."

"Well, I don't know about lightning bolts, but the way you hit him in that flying tackle was pretty damn impressive. If a body blow like that isn't judgment from above, I don't know what is. You took that rat bastard down *hard*." She actually blushed and turned her face away with a sheepish grin.

"I love you both so damn much, I'm stupid with it." Ziporah turned back to him with a full-blown smile on her beautiful, flushed face. "That makes three of us."

"Yeah," Cami chimed in, "three of us." Then Evan took a note from Ziporah's playbook and tackled them both into the couch. The laughter and affection they shared in that moment brought hope to all of them. The shadows of the past faced and conquered. Like the dawn breaking from a long dark night, there was only healing and light for the three of them now, at last.

Chapter Thirty-One

Evan checked one last time to make sure everything was ready in his office before he hit the intercom. "Okay Tanner you can send him in." Staying in his seat and maintaining a calm and professional exterior was one of the hardest things Evan had ever done in his life as Mark Wahlberg walked into his office and faced him.

"Look man," Mark said, taking the lead by making a slashing movement with his right hand as though to clear the slate. "I'm sorry you had to see that. I hope you don't think I go around hitting on random women in bars." He held up both hands at his sides, and scrunched his face up in a *'what can you do'* expression.

"The sad truth is, I've got history with those two, and it was just a sorry turn of events that you had to be there to witness it." Evan nodded his head and tried to make his expression appear sympathetic and thoughtful, as he thought to himself *keep talking, asshole, just keep talkin'*.

"Why don't you have a seat and tell me about it?" Evan asked, while visions of strangling the man with his bare hands danced through his mind.

"Well, it's personal, and its old history that just came out of nowhere. So, if it's all the same to you, I'd like to talk business and leave the personal out of it."

I bet you would jerk-off, but that's not gonna happen.

"Oh, but it isn't the same to me. You see, as I've told you on several occasions, my business is personal, so before we take this further I'd like to know what happened." Evan watched Mark process that and sit back in his chair. He could almost see the wheels spinning behind the other man's eyes, as he scrambled for a way to get out of it.

"You know how it is, back in high school and college. You remember how the girls were, right?" Evan felt bile boil in his stomach, and managed to make a noncommittal grunt that Mark took as agreement. "Yeah. They were all drunk on the power of brand-new boobs, and the ability to lead a guy around by his dick. But then, after you dump your whole paycheck on 'em and get them alone, they pull out the scared virgin act." Mark was either oblivious or blind, that he failed to pick up on the rage he was enticing out of Evan, because he leaned forward and warmed to his story, nodding his head to emphasize his point.

"Being a wrestler, I was a pretty big deal at high school, so that happened there a lot." Mark rolled his eyes. "Cheerleaders, right?" Then he looked back at Evan and shook his head as though baffled. "So there I was in college on a wrestling scholarship, and along comes this hot little blonde. I tailed her for a month. And she liked it, she liked the attention, she liked me. She liked me so much that on our first date, she even let me take her out into the middle of nowhere."

Mark was so zealous about the subject that he leaned forward and braced his elbow on Evan's desk and pointed a finger at him. "We get there, and the place is closed up tight. But does she complain then? Does she ask me to take her home? No. Not once. She follows me out into the middle of a God damn cornfield, in the middle of the God damn night, and then tries to act like she doesn't know what's going to God damn happen once we get there."

With a flounce, Mark sat back in his seat and slapped the arms of his chair in disgust. "Well, it was bullshit. She was all over me, and kissing me, with her tongue halfway down my throat. She had this great rack that she was rubbing all over me, and I was just a kid. You know how it was back then. Young, dumb and full of cum, right?" He gave what Evan could only assume was a good old boy chuckle at that witty comment, and then continued. "Well she got what she was asking for, and yeah, maybe it was a little rough, but hey, it was hot and she liked it. Then, the next day the stupid bitch cried rape." Now the look that came over Mark's face was a self-satisfied smile that had Evan seeing red.

"It wasn't. No way in hell was it. She wouldn't let it drop, though. And took it all the way to fucking court. There I was on a full-ride scholarship, my whole life ahead of me, and this little piece of tail who had morning-after regrets has me up on trial. Can you believe that shit?" As a matter of fact, Evan thought, I can't believe this shit at all. But Evan didn't say a word for now, no matter that the urge to kill the man was so strong, every muscle in his body trembled with it.

"Well, the court saw the truth and let me go. Not guilty. Because that's what I was. *I was not guilty.* But I got punished anyway." He whined. "I lost my scholarship and got kicked out of school. I didn't get to wrestle anymore, not when they found out I'd been using steroids. I had dreams about that, about my wrestling. And because of one piece of ass, I lost it, lost my chance at ever wrestling again. But that's in the past, and I let it go and never thought about it again. Until I walked into the bar and saw her working there."

Mark looked at Evan, and Evan could see him trying to put an earnest expression on his face. "I didn't start nothing with those girls. I would've left well enough alone even after all they cost me. Because the dark-haired one is the blonde's best friend and she was pre-law so I'm sure it was her that made Cami go to the cops. But that's neither here nor there, I would have let them be. They were the ones that came after me. I was just defending myself.

"You know, come to think of it, I don't think I should leave it at that now. I'm not sure if they both worked there, but after all that little blonde has cost me, I think I'm going to put a phone call into her boss. It would be interesting to see what he thinks about her attacking a paying customer."

Evan figured he'd heard enough. And even if he hadn't, he couldn't stomach another word out of the smug bastards lying face. "Well, as far as putting a phone call into the owner of one of New York's most popular and successful new taverns, I'm afraid you might want to rethink that. You see, Cami owns that place, so it wouldn't do you any good." The angry flush that started at the base of Mark's throat was a satisfying start, but Evan wasn't nearly finished with him yet.

"And let's see," Evan pretended to ponder with a finger on his chin and a wrinkle between his brows. "High school and college girls. You asked me if I remembered what they were like," Evan said, dropping the pretense to look at him with contempt.

"I remember them as innocent and beautiful as brand-new foals. I remember them to be delightful and charming and fragile, and as far as I know, that still holds true today." Unable to sit still any longer, Evan pushed to his feet and braced both hands on his desk as he loomed into Mark's personal space.

"Now, as for the night you brutally raped my future wife, I have a hell of a lot to say about that. But every word of it could be best said with the end of my fist. Let me assure you, you miserable son of a bitch, once you leave this office, your get out of jail free card is expired. I suggest you run far and you run fast, because I'm going to be coming for you, and you are not going to like the results." Mark must've heard the deadly resolve in Evan's voice, because his charm and his easy-going manner deserted him and left him sitting there as what he was at his core. A coward.

Evan had to force himself to sit back down, because every cell in his body wanted to dismantle the man across from him piece by piece. "After Friday night, I started researching you. Looking deeper into you and not just your company. You may be interested to know that I woke up all five of our lawyers, and they have been looking into those sexual harassment lawsuits that you had filed against you over the last years. With the information that I was able to give them, I believe those girls are going to be getting quite a boost in their settlements now that they all know about each other." Evan took grim satisfaction from the way Mark paled as all the blood drained from his face.

"Now then where does that leave us, hmm?" Evan asked in a mock singsong voice. "Oh yes, reputation. I've been telling you all these weeks how important my reputation and the reputation of my company is to me. And I believed you, when you told me your reputation and the reputation of your family's company was equally important to you. So I hope this hurts like a son of a bitch." Evan turned his laptop around, and watched Mark gasp like a fish on a hook to see what was on his screen.

The satellite conference call had been activated, and every company that Pac-West had dealings with was there, and had been watching their entire exchange.

"From the looks on those faces, I'd say your reputation is shot. What do you think?" Evan asked, as though it was a serious question. The triumphant pleasure he felt in that moment was only a fraction of what he would get from ripping the asshole limb from limb but he'd take what he could get.

"You mother fucker." Angry red flushed up his neck and over his cheeks as Mark surged to his feet. "You God damned mother fucker. My own shareholders and board members are on there, too!" Mark shouted, staring at the screen in furious dismay. "You can't get away with this shit. This is slander or entrapment or something. I'm going to sue you, you prick! I didn't give you permission to record this meeting! This will never hold up in a court." Evan sat back in his chair and made a come on gesture with one hand.

"Sue me. Try it, I dare you. No I beg you. You see, I didn't record this, I just broadcast it. Although, in all fairness, since it was broadcast, anybody watching could have recorded it and probably did. Something else to consider, the other love of my life, and also future wife, the brunette? She did finish law school, and has assured me that in the state of New York, I could, in fact, record this conversation without your knowledge if I had wanted to. So, if you want to go to court and make this public record, by all means, let's do." Mark howled in rage, and moved as though to attack, and Evan delighted in the other man's impotent fury. He stayed where he was, but had every muscle in his body ready and eager to counter his assault.

"Mark!" The disembodied shout stopped the man mid-lunge, as though a leash had been yanked. "Get your stupid ass out of there now." Mark didn't move, with the exception of his eyes that darted from the laptop to Evan, as rage turned his handsome face a mottled purple mess. "I'm not going to tell you again, son. Get out. Get on a plane. And get home, so your mother and I can figure out what the hell to do with you now."

"Uh-oh Markey," Evan said with his eyes glued to the other man's. "Daddy's pissed. Better run home. I think you're grounded."

Chapter Thirty-Two

"Say it again, please, please, pretty please." Cami was bouncing in her seat as she tugged on the front of Evan's sweatshirt. "Just one more time, say it for me because you love me."

"I think you're grounded," Evan repeated for what felt like the millionth time, and both women dissolved into laughter yet again. "I don't know why you keep asking me to tell you what happened when you both watched the whole thing."

"Yeah," Z said as she wiped tears from her eyes, and tucked her chilly feet underneath his thigh, "but it's not the same as hearing you tell it. It was on the computer, so we didn't get the real nuances of everything."

"And you sound so sexy when you say it. And you looked so sexy when you said it back then. So I think I need to hear it, just one more time." Evan groaned, wrapped his arms around her and pulled pulling her in for a long tongue-thrusting kiss in hopes of getting her mind off of the subject. The girls had recorded it so they could play it back anytime they wanted to. And they'd been talking about it for hours already. As far as Evan was concerned, today's events were not enough, it would never be enough, but it was enough for now, so he was tired of dwelling on it. Besides, he would much rather spend the evening making love to the women who owned his heart.

"So, come on, tell us again how you showed that *schmuck* what was what."

Z squealed when Evan whipped out a hand, folded her over his knee and landed a good hard slap to her ass. When he brought her up and held her nose to nose with him, it was hard for him to keep a straight face. She looked shocked, appalled and also turned on. "Sugar," he said in his best Dom voice, "I may be from Texas, but I've been in New York long enough to know what that word means, and that no sub of mine should be saying it." Then he kissed the tip of her nose and added with a smile, "So, I'll say it for you. He *is* a schmuck." Delighted, she laughed and gave him a loud smacking kiss before sitting back again.

Evan knew that the Wahlbergs would scramble in an effort to save their company, but that meeting had dealt them a crippling blow and it would be a miracle if they survived. In the seven years since Cami's attack, Mark's parents had made over a dozen sexual complaints about their son disappear. Their long string of success in doing so owed mostly to a lot of money and nondisclosure agreements.

While those nondisclosure agreements pertained only to the victims not talking, they couldn't do anything about stopping others from talking. After today, they all knew about each other, and the two that were still pending had just been lined up for even bigger paydays. Evan hoped fervently that they moved from class action to criminal with this new information, but whether or not they did was out of his hands.

As for his own company, Evan had convinced the Board to take on the expense of keeping the distribution in-house. He shuddered to think what those lawsuits would have done to his family's company had they not found this out ahead of time. No amount of money was worth a risk like that.

"Sweet brat," Evan said and placed a tender kiss on the tip of her nose. "Can you let it go now? At least for tonight? Thinking about that man and what happened makes me want to hunt him down and kill him." Her hands cupped his cheeks, and she made a sort of cooing sound, like what women usually reserve for small babies.

"Of course we can, my Sir," she said in a ridiculous baby voice as she kissed him on his nose. "On two conditions … You say it just one more time. And then we watch Buffy." Evan growled and dropped his head to the back of the couch in defeat. "I think you're grounded."

Ziporah whooped and launched herself toward the kitchen. "I'll get the chocolate cake shots, wahoo!"

"At least I can get drunk." Both women laughed, and Cami rained sweet, adoring kisses across his face as he wrapped his arms around her and held tight.

Epilogue

Eleven months later, it was a warm September afternoon. Texas had decided to smile on them as Evan stood in the shade of the giant oak tree in his family's backyard, the leaves on it the brilliant golds, oranges, and browns of sunset. There were flowers everywhere; sunflowers and Gerber daisies in every fall shade were draped over everything in sight.

When choosing the date had come up, it was Cami who had picked the fall. She wanted to reclaim it, once and for all. Harvest was a time to gather all from the past and reap the rewards of it, then clear away the unwanted to make room for new beginnings. What better time for them to do that than in the fall, she'd asked, and both himself and Z had agreed whole-heartedly.

They were both taking his name, which shocked the hell out of him. He hadn't expected it, especially from Ziporah, but they'd told him that, although they had wills and this commitment ceremony binding them, they wanted his name as well. All three of them, united in every way possible.

Gage stood at his left as he fussed with his tie and tried to remain calm. There were more than a hundred people here today, even though they had tried to keep the event small. However, between the three of them, there were a lot of people that loved them and wanted to be here to show their support.

A commitment ceremony wasn't a marriage in the eyes of the law, but the commitment was binding and real just the same. He was taking them as wife and they were taking him as husband, and it felt like the most natural thing in the world.

The girls each had their own wedding set. He had delighted them with a surprise trip to Tiffany's and told them the sky was the limit. Cami chose a princess cut–why was he not surprised–set with a one-carat flawless diamond in the center and two half-carat ones on either side of it, with a wedding band that was a full circle of inset smaller ones.

Z had picked out a round diamond that was also a full carat. Her nod to the symbolism of the three of them was how the engagement ring fit within the wedding band. It had a fan of diamonds on either side of the sole diamond that surrounded the stone with brilliance.

Evan had his rings specially made. His band was an interlocking one that came in two rings that each woman would place on his finger. It was a design that, once the two fit together, would look like a band made of three white gold strands woven together, inseparable and infinite.

The music started and Evan stood a little straighter, held his shoulders back and his head high. He was flooded with pride and wonder at the vision that was floating toward him.

Cami's dress brushed the ground in front of her as she walked and had a small train trailing behind. It wasn't quite white in color, and the material had a shimmer to it. Over the top of it was a chiffon layer that was dripping with tiny sparkling gems that caught in the sunlight from every direction and made her glow.

It had a sweetheart neckline that displayed her breasts to mouth-watering perfection, and draped off her shoulders and down her back in a waterfall of sparkles. All her lovely hair was piled on top of her head in fat, shiny curls, with a real diamond tiara at the base of them.

Ziporah's dress was in that same almost white shade and it too had a train. But her train was long; it dragged behind her regally with every step she took. There were no gemstones sweetly sewn into her dress, instead the shimmer came from the fabric itself as it flowed around her, almost like liquid, as she moved.

With an empire waistline that showcased her trim build, she looked like Audrey Hepburn and Grace Kelly floating down the aisle. She'd grown her hair out and pulled it up as well, only instead of curls it was in a sleek twist. And in place of a tiara, there was a diamond clip at the crown of her head, with a small thin veil that trailed down her back and along her train.

As soon as they reached him, Evan stepped between Cami and Z then took his place. When they faced each other and recited the vows that they had written themselves, Evan felt tears and laughter threatening. His life had been full before he'd walked into Cami's bar that night. He had a wonderful family that he adored. A job at the helm of his family's empire and a strong connection with a tight-knit group of friends he trusted and loved. He hadn't known what true happiness was though, not really. Life had a richness to it now that he'd never known was possible. It was like he'd been living in black and white until they brought color to his world. *They* were his life now. His happiness was irrevocably tied-up with theirs. Every sadness that life brought their way would be faced and weathered together. Miraculous was too small a word for the breadth and scope of what he was feeling in that moment, but that's what they were to him, *miraculous*.

Ziporah was vowing to love him as long as he breathed, and to stop that breathing should he ever stray. Sweet Cami vowed to sing to him when he was sick, comfort him when he was sad, and put up with him when he watched football.

In return, standing on his family's land under the tree his ancestors had planted, Evan vowed to give them everything. His heart, his soul, and, with a wink for Z, even his very breath.

He was theirs, he told them, he had been theirs from the start, and he was going to spend the rest of his life loving them. "And to sum up, I'd like to quote the immortal words of Spike, amended just a bit to fit you two. 'When I say, "I love you," it's not just because I want you both. It has nothing to do with me. I love what you are, Ziporah, what you do, and how hard you try. I've seen your kindness, Cami, and your strength. I've seen the best and the worst of you both. And I understand with perfect clarity exactly who and what you both are. You're each a hell of a woman."

Then, for Z and her beloved bubbe, Evan placed the crystal goblet within its satin bag on the ground at his feet and crushed it. The Jewish symbol of breaking with the old and starting with the new, and the same reason Cami had chosen the fall for their ceremony. As the satisfying sound filled the air, he gathered his brides close and finished. "You're it for me. You're the ones–my own Buffys."

When his brides burst into delighted laughter, Evan could only guess that the people who laughed with them were more Joss Whedon fans.

EMBRACING THE FALL

As they kissed, with his hands cupping the backs of their heads, he could hear the cheers and applause of their families and friends, and at that moment, as though it was a blessing from above, the sun broke through the leaves overhead. Evan felt the dazzling rays bathing them in its warm embrace, and it seemed to chase every shadow of the past away with a promise of only light from this day forward.

The End

About the Author

Lainey lives in beautiful Lake Stevens with her daughter and their many pets. When Lainey isn't writing or reading she enjoys cooking for her friends, going to the theater or movies and exploring the nature hikes in the Cascade Mountains. For more on Lainey, visit her website: www.laineyreese.com or her Facebook page.

Other Titles by Lainey Reese

The New York series
A Table For Three
Damaged Goods
Innocence Defied

~ Novellas ~
Snowfall
Guarding Nadia